### *"You okay?" Carter's lips lightly feathered hers as he spoke.*

Georgia took a deep breath and nodded. Better than okay. She was perfect. Pulsing. Alive. Able to leap tall buildings in a single bound.

"Good." Forehead to forehead, he stood with her for a moment, his eyes closed. "Wow," he murmured.

"Mmm. Wow." Her nose brushed his as she nodded.

A tiny smile touched his lips and he sighed. "C'mon. We gotta get out of here."

Not sure if this was because they were being pursued or because he wanted privacy, Georgia didn't know or care. "Mmm." Arms dangling, head spinning, she simply stood there, dazed.

Cootie Biggles had just kissed her.

And she would never be the same again.

Dear Reader,

In this month of tricks or treats, there's no magic to delivering must-read love stories each month. We simply publish upbeat stories from the heart and hope you find them a treat.

**What can you do to keep these great stories coming? Plenty! You can write me or visit our online community at www.eHarlequin.com and let me know the stories you like best. Or if you have trouble finding the latest Silhouette Romance titles, be sure to remind your local bookseller how much you enjoy them. This way you will never miss your favorites.**

For example, IN A FAIRY TALE WORLD… combines classic love stories, a matchmaking princess and a sprinkling of fairy-tale magic for all-out fun! Myrna Mackenzie launches this Silhouette Romance six-book series with *Their Little Cowgirl* (#1738)—the story of a cowboy and urban Cinderella who lock horns and then hearts over his darling baby daughter.

In *Georgia Gets Her Groom!* (#1739), the latest in Carolyn Zane's THE BRUBAKER BRIDES series, Georgia discovers that Mr. Wrong might be the right man for her, after all. Then watch what happens when a waitress learns her new ranch hand is a tycoon in disguise, in *The Billionaire's Wedding Masquerade* (#1740) by Melissa McClone. And if you like feisty heroines and the wealthy heroes that sweep them off their feet, you'll want to read *Cinderella's Lucky Ticket* by Melissa James (#1741).

Read these romance treats and share the love and laughter with Silhouette Romance this month!

Mavis C. Allen
Associate Senior Editor, Silhouette Romance

Please address questions and book requests to:
Silhouette Reader Service
U.S.: 3010 Walden Ave., P.O. Box 1325, Buffalo, NY 14269
Canadian: P.O. Box 609, Fort Erie, Ont. L2A 5X3

# Georgia Gets Her Groom!

## CAROLYN ZANE

SILHOUETTE *Romance*®

Published by Silhouette Books

**America's Publisher of Contemporary Romance**

For Melissa Jeglinski and Amy Tannenbaum—
two very talented young women from whom I am always
learning. Thank you for being my "guardian editors."
*Psalms* 117:2

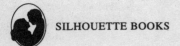 SILHOUETTE BOOKS

ISBN 0-373-19739-X

GEORGIA GETS HER GROOM!

Copyright © 2004 by Carolyn Pizzuti

This edition published by arrangement with Harlequin Books S.A.

Visit Silhouette Books at www.eHarlequin.com

**Printed in U.S.A.**

## CAROLYN ZANE

lives with her husband, Matt, and their three children in the rolling countryside near Portland, Oregon's Willamette River. Like Chevy Chase's character in the movie *Funny Farm,* Carolyn finally decided to trade in a decade of city dwelling and producing local television commercials for the quaint country life of a novelist. And, even though they have bitten off decidedly more than they can chew in the remodeling of their hundred-plus-year-old farmhouse, life is somewhat saner for her than for poor Chevy. The neighbors are friendly, the mail carrier actually stops at the box and the dog, Bob Barker, sticks close to home.

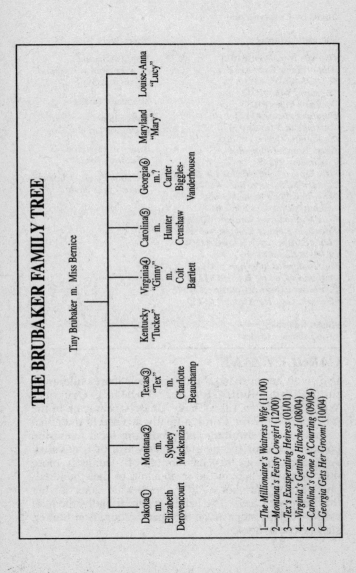

# THE BRUBAKER FAMILY TREE

Tiny Brubaker m. Miss Bernice

Dakota① m. Elizabeth Derovencourt

Montana② m. Sydney Mackenzie

Texas③ "Tex" m. Charlotte Beauchamp

Kentucky "Tucker"

Virginia④ "Ginny" m. Colt Bartlett

Carolina⑤ m. Hunter Crenshaw

Georgia⑥ m.? Carter Biggles-Vanderhousen

Maryland "Mary"

Louise-Anna "Lucy"

1—*The Millionaire's Waitress Wife* (11/00)
2—*Montana's Feisty Cowgirl* (12/00)
3—*Tex's Exasperating Heiress* (01/01)
4—*Virginia's Getting Hitched* (08/04)
5—*Carolina's Gone A'Courting* (09/04)
6—*Georgia Gets Her Groom!* (10/04)

# *Chapter One*

"What is it, darling? You look positively...pasty."

Georgia Brubaker snapped shut her cell phone and bestowed her new boyfriend, Brandon McGraw, with a wan smile. "I'm so sorry, honey, but that was my aunt Clarise. She sounded a tad frantic. It seems that some guests have begun to arrive prematurely back at the Circle BO and I'm being called to action."

"But, snookie-cookie—" Brandon's silly, seesawing brows made her smile "—you only just got here."

"I know, but duty calls." Georgia's smile faded and she sighed as she tucked her phone away and began to gather her purse and jacket. "Among several other overeager families, the Biggles-Vanderhousens are here in Texas, back from their home on the French Riviera, and it seems that this time, they've brought their—" her nose wrinkled in distaste "—son."

Georgia's shoulders drooped, mirroring the corners of

her mouth. How disappointing. She and Brandon had planned to spend the summer afternoon in the cool luxury of his baronial-style library, relaxing over a game of chess and listening to his extensive collection of classical music. Not exactly the most exhilarating activity she could imagine, but it seemed pleasant enough, and besides, it gave her more time to get to know Brandon better. On a very cerebral level, she felt Brandon embodied all the qualities that would make him "the one" for her. However, her three-month-long vacation seemed to be speeding to its conclusion, and she would be heading back home to Oklahoma sans engagement ring by the end of the summer if they didn't kick-start this late-in-the-day romance into high gear.

Unlike her sisters before her, Georgia wasn't a believer in letting *this* perfectly good fish wriggle off the line.

Wringing her hands over the inept timing of the Biggles-Vanderhousen family's appearance, she glanced with longing at the slender flute of champagne and the silver platter spread with an assortment of imported cheeses and a loaf of crusty French bread. Her stomach growled in protest as she stood to leave.

Brandon rose to his own feet and helped her sort out her lacy summer jacket. His tone was teasing as he guided her arms through the filmy sleeves. "I'm not sure I understand what their son has to do with you, Georgia. Should I be jealous?"

Horrified laughter bubbled forth as she spun around to face him. "No! Oh, please, no. He is the *last* person on earth you should fear—" she paused and tossed him a saucy grin "—absconding with my affections. No, this weeklong 'family' reunion that Big Daddy and Miss Clarise are throwing includes everyone from here to the Oklahoma panhandle. And those are just the Brubaker relatives," she said with a laugh. Everyone in Hidden Valley, Texas, knew that Big Daddy Brubaker and his siblings had raised huge families. And now that their offspring were marrying and having children of their own, the clan was growing by leaps and bounds.

Since this was the summer Georgia and two of her sisters, Ginny and Carolina, had all managed to have the same time off, they'd come to spend the time relaxing with her lovable uncle and his wife at their ranch before they all became too busy with their chosen careers, although Georgia had yet to figure out what to do with her business degrees. It had been lazy and wonderful, and—for her sisters at any rate—filled with life-changing love.

Sliding a hand under her hair, Georgia freed it from where it was trapped by her jacket and gave her head a tiny shake. "Plus, 'business relations' such as the Biggles-Vanderhousens make up another hoard. There is no way my aunt can play hostess to everyone, so she divvied up the masses, and the Biggles-Vanderhousens ended up on my list." Her lips pruned.

"That's a powerful family name in these parts. You don't care for them?"

"Oh, it's not that. Mr. and Mrs. Biggles-Vanderhousen are very nice. It's just—" she squeezed her eyes shut and grimaced "—as a child I was regularly commandeered into playing with their loathsome little boy. At any rate, Miss Clarise tells me they are suffering from jet lag and feels they'd do well with a family member to provide the personal touch. Since my sisters are both newly married, that leaves me. As my aunt and uncle have been so gracious and generous, I feel it's the least I can do."

"You know—" Brandon stroked his jaw "—I think I remember a Biggles-Vanderhousen boy from my school. He was a number of years younger than me. Puny, bespectacled runt of a kid. Bad at polo. Bad at cricket. Bad at lacrosse. Bad at tennis. Even bad at the more bohemian sports such as baseball," he mused as he squinted off into his boyhood at prep school. "As I recall, some of the guys would stuff him into a locker now and again…"

Georgia's exhalation was long and slow. "That's him."

"Computer genius, right?"

"Yes," she groaned. "The family lives in France most of the year but still winters at their Big V spread just up the road a piece."

"Right. I know the place. So, tell me, aside from being a bit of a dork, why did you find this kid so loathsome?"

Georgia did her best to briefly explain as they strolled from the library and into the hall. "When I was a kid—before we moved to Oklahoma from Texas—my family was nearly always at my uncle's place, as we lived so close and all. Anyhow, more times than I care to remember, Mr. Biggles-Vanderhousen would drop by the ranch on business, always towing his weird little boy whose name was, uh, er, oh…shoot…" She frowned and searched her brain. "For some reason I can't remember his first name. All of us kids called him Cootie."

"That was nice of you." Brandon lifted a censorious brow that had Georgia's cheeks coloring.

"Yes, well, we were immature. Anyway, since I had the misfortune to be the same age as little, uh, you know, Cootie, I was expected to entertain him. And, since the Biggles-Vanderhousen family is very prominent, not only in Hidden Valley, Texas, but also in the worldwide oil community, there was no ditching him. The backlash would have been catastrophic on a global level. Or so they led me to believe."

Brandon's chuckle rumbled.

"And now I must go welcome him back to Hidden Valley and make him feel at home. I can barely believe that I haven't seen any of them in more than a decade."

"Perhaps Cootie has changed for the better?"

"I wish, but I have to believe it would be virtually impossible. Worse yet, Miss Clarise just requested that I be his personal hostess all week. No doubt because he's still socially inept."

"Poor darling. You," he clarified, grinning, "not him." Brandon captured her hands in his and swung them to and fro. "What can I do to help?"

Lips at full pout, Georgia peeked up at Brandon in her most coquettish manner. "Promise me that you will never leave my side, for the entire duration of the reunion."

Brandon drew her into his arms and murmured into her ear. "Consider it done."

"Promise?" Georgia held out her little finger. "Pinkie-swear?"

Threading his pinkie through hers, Brandon promised. "I'll play your ardent lover at every turn for an entire week."

"Thank you," Georgia whispered in relief.

"You're welcome." Voice turning husky, Brandon nuzzled Georgia's nose with his own. "In fact, I think we should start practicing our PDAs now."

"Our what?"

"'Public displays of affection.' Don't you think we should," he lifted a roguish brow, "rehearse a little bit now, just so we'll seem completely natural when the time comes?"

Gracious. Did that include kisses? Embarrassed, she glanced at him. His expression held that promise.

"*P-D-A!* Oh! Right! Of course!" Unprepared for his plan, Georgia swallowed a sudden bout of butterflies. "Practice makes perfect, as they say."

Though they'd been dating for nearly two weeks now, because of either bad timing or lack of privacy Brandon had yet to give Georgia more than a chaste peck on the cheek and a lingering hug at the end of each date. And now, here it was. The moment she'd been dreaming of.

They were alone, she had the time and *Brandon McGraw was going to kiss her.* Properly. On the mouth. So that when other people watched them kissing, they would look…natural.

Eyes blinking like the shutter on a camera, she ran her tongue over her teeth and prayed that they were squeaky clean and her breath sweet. Her heart picked up speed as she angled her head to match the tilt of his. Lips looming, Georgia felt her eyes cross before they slid closed. At contact, her erratic pulses slowed, and then…returned to normal.

*Hmm,* Georgia thought after a moment. *Peculiar.*

As his lips settled upon hers and began to move rhythmically back and forth, she felt…well…oddly, she felt…nothing. It was as if she'd stepped outside of her body and was viewing the unfolding scene from a distance. What was happening seemed for all the world to be natural and exciting and intimate, but in actuality it was just four lips, sliding about with no particular agenda.

How strange.

Where were the fireworks she'd anticipated all her life? Where was the raging heartbeat? The labored breathing? The moaning in ecstasy? Certainly there was no chemical explosion on her part.

It was her fault.

Had to be.

She'd never been good at simply being "in" the moment. She was always next to it, outside it, in the vicinity of it, but never, ever "in" the moment. Always analyzing, thinking too much, unable to just relax and enjoy. What was wrong with her? Why were all of her friends able to get carried away and float among the clouds during moments such as this? And here she was, listening to that little whistle in Brandon's nose as he puffed away on her face.

She wondered what was going on in Brandon's head.

The moist tip of his tongue rimmed her lips, and Georgia tried to remember if she'd packed a tissue in her purse. And a lipstick. She gave herself a mental shake. What was she doing?

Brandon was *kissing* her for crying in the night, and she was busy feeling...slobbered upon. Resounding smacks and slurps echoed in the library and to her horror, she suddenly felt a roaring case of the giggles well in her throat.

*Uh-oh.*

Digging her fingernails into her palms to forestall the sonic blast she felt building, Georgia pleaded with herself not to give in to this onslaught of nervous laughter now. How completely inappropriate. How horrifying. But the more she warned herself not to, the more desperate became the need to laugh.

*Smack. Slurp. Smack.*

*No! Stop it! I will not laugh. I will not laugh.* Tears sprang to her eyes as she ground the heel of her shoe into her toe. Such an odd thing, kissing. So much loud smacking and slurping. Of their own volition, her lips curved and she battled them back to the task at hand. When that didn't work, she redoubled her efforts with the heel of her shoe until her toe was badly bruised. Maybe even broken. Oh, that hurt like a son of a gun. Still, she wanted to laugh.

*Kiss him. Just grow up and do it.*

Circling Brandon's neck with her arms, she plunged her hands into his perfectly groomed hair and worked at building up a sweat. She tried to feel the vibe, to experience the thrill, but strangely all that came was an even more frantic need to laugh. To laugh the kind of thigh-slapping, tear-streaming, belly-busting laughter that always got her into terrible trouble as a child. Determined to conquer both her laughter and Brandon, she snuggled ever closer and focused on converting her mirth into sexual energy.

Georgia desperately wanted this to work.

Brandon had all the qualities of her perfect match.

She also harbored a niggling desire to succeed where both of her sisters had failed in their own relationships with Brandon. It was both illogical and idiotic, Georgia knew. But it was there.

An ugly competitive streak.

She hated that, in herself. Although, to be honest, this jealousy was nothing new. All her life, Georgia had felt overshadowed by her two older, successful, charismatic, adventurous sisters. Compared to them, she felt the veritable slug.

Her oldest sister, Virginia, had the brains. As a psychologist, she worked in a field that excited her and allowed her to give something important back to the public. To ice that perfect cake, she'd married one of Big Daddy's ranch hands, Colt Bartlett, this summer and was now expecting a baby.

Carolina, on the other hand, had the personality and was as high spirited as she was creative. And she was still exuding that annoying honeymoon glow with her new husband, Hunt Crenshaw, also one of Big Daddy's hands.

As for herself? Georgia felt that all she had going for her were dreams. Dreams of adventure. Romance. Excitement. However, if those things were what she truly wanted, what was wrong with her now? Here she was, being kissed by an exceedingly handsome, endlessly sweet, disgustingly rich dreamboat, and not a single tingle of adventure, romance or excitement tiptoed down her spine.

Instead she got nervous laughter out of the deal.

Disgusted with her apparent immaturity, Georgia was determined to enjoy herself as much as her sisters seemed to enjoy their new husbands. Eyes narrowed, jaw firm with resolve, Georgia kneaded Brandon's scalp with her fingertips and converted her misplaced emotion into some shrill moans. After all, didn't her sister Dr. Ginny always say, "If one 'acts' the part, one will begin to 'feel' the part?"

After she'd completed the requisite hair plunging, she raked her hands from Brandon's head to his chest where she performed some enthusiastic massage. Unfortunately, a button or two popped off his shirt and went pinging to the floor.

"Sorry." Mortified, she choked back another round of giggles and bit her upper lip as she smoothed his torn placket. Okay, so forget chest massage. Switching gears, she focused on running the toe of her shoe up and down his pant leg with vigor.

*"Yesssss,"* she hissed and, gripping his shoulders, arched back and wondered whether if she spoke Spanish she'd be hissing *"Siiiiii!"* Or if she were French, *"Ouiiiii!"*

*Weeeeeeeeeeeee!!*

She was for sure going to lose it now. Rear molars closed on a bit of her cheek till she drew blood and she cried out in pain. Through the fringe of her lashes, she cracked her eyelids open to peer at Brandon's reaction. Warped by both proximity and angle, his face looked as if he were standing behind a huge fishbowl, distorted and dazed. His hair stood on end from her energetic efforts. Looking down, she could see that the legs of his pants were covered with scuffmarks.

*Ohhhhhhh,* she had to get out of here.

Now.

"*Ohhhhhhh,* yes. I mean, no! No, no, no. I have to be going," she said huskily, and hoped she exuded a reluctance to leave rather than a blossoming need to drop to the floor and howl at the ceiling.

Seemingly shell-shocked by what had just transpired, Brandon released her and took a wobbly step back. "Oh. Right. I guess so. Sure."

"Mmm. Yes." Georgia whirled on her heel, waved and hobbled on her sore toes across the massive foyer to pull open the front door. "But I'll be back just as soon as I get the Biggles-Vanderhousens squared away. Maybe late tonight we can sneak off for a private dinner and drinks? Practice our public displays of affection some more?" Ohhh, yeah. They needed some serious practice. Perhaps some time spent with the boring Biggles-Vanderhousen boy would put her in a sober frame of mind.

"I…uh, okay," Brandon stared down at his torn shirt pocket and the holes where his buttons used to be and then shot her a curious glance. "I'll see you later."

As Georgia sped down the long, ruler-straight road toward her uncle's ranch, she fumbled through her purse and extracted the personal party planner that Miss Clarise had printed up especially for this unprecedented soirée. The party was intended to celebrate the summer's conclusion, yes, but more importantly it was meant to double as a reception to honor the marriages of both Virginia and Carolina.

Absolutely amazing.

Georgia shook her head. Who'd have guessed that when Miss Clarise invited Georgia and her sisters to visit the Circle BO for some postgrad R&R earlier that summer, her sisters would find the men of their dreams, right here in Hidden Valley, Texas? Now they would be staying on at the Circle BO with their macho husbands and living dream lives.

Feeling morose, Georgia stared out the windshield as the miles sped beneath her tires. What a loser. If things didn't work out with Brandon—and she had to wonder after her sordid display just now—Georgia would head home to Oklahoma where it seemed all she could anticipate was a humdrum life in the family oil business. Without her sisters. Without marriage prospects. Without her dreams.

Unknowingly Miss Clarise had sprinkled Georgia's wounds with salt when she'd enlisted her help to make the guest lists, assign tasks and act as her personal assistant. After all, since Georgia was unmarried, she'd have more time to devote to helping organize the party.

Eyes half on the road and half on the task at hand, she flipped through the pages till she reached the first week in August. There it was. Her guest list. And there he was.

Little Cootie Biggles.

Aka Carter Biggles-Vanderhousen. *Carter.* Right. *That* was his first name. She'd never be able to think of him as anything but Cootie. And, though Georgia liked to believe that she'd never looked down on any person because of a few character quirks, back in the old days little Cootie was just too weird for words.

The blurry past came into focus as she stared at the pulsing white stripe in the middle of the road. Suddenly there she was, back in kindergarten, sitting at the desk she shared with tiny, toothless Cootie. What was it exactly that had turned her off? And at such an age of innocence? She mulled over the possibilities.

It hadn't been the fact that he was in continual need of

a tissue. Georgia had been able to overlook a serious case of postnasal drip. Neither was it the missing front teeth that caused him to shower his listener with spittle as he stuttered and lisped his way through a conversation. She hadn't even held against Cootie the time back at age four, when he'd lost control of his bladder, so great was his interest in an ant farm the preschool teacher had brought to show the class. Although she'd never worn those patent-leather Mary Janes again.

No, it wasn't the continually soiled clothes, the socks that didn't match or the tangles in the back of his wispy, flyaway hair that made him a veritable Charles Schulz-esque Pig Pen, in spite of his mother's—and all of his nannies'—best efforts. In fact, there was no particular thing, really, one could pinpoint about Cootie that made him so incredibly unpopular.

It was simply a compilation of…everything.

Summer after summer, from the age of three to eight, Georgia had tried—for the sake of peace in the international oil community—to find something, *anything,* endearing about Cootie. But she could not.

Lord knew she'd tried.

In day camp, she'd tattled on the bullies who'd beaten him half-senseless. In kindergarten, she'd put up with him—and several painful injuries—when he'd been assigned as her dance partner for the parents' pageant. She'd taped his glasses back together on more than one occasion and pinched his nose shut to keep him from bleeding half to death every time he fell off the monkey bars.

Blessedly, when Georgia entered the third grade, her parents moved to their oil fields in Oklahoma and she hadn't seen Cootie since. Still, the sour taste in her mouth lingered.

And now she was stuck with good old Cootie and his family at the season's biggest party in Texas.

Her speed increased with her irritation. Blast it all anyway, this was her chance to shine for Brandon. She was single, available and, with the dresses she'd had made by some of the world's top designers, beautiful. She didn't want to spend the evening pinching Cootie's nose shut and defending his right to hold a conversation, no matter how dull.

"I can't be everywhere at once," the genteel Miss Clarise had softly explained. "Show them around. Make 'em feel at home. I know how much your mama and papa adore the Biggles-Vanderhousens, so you might draw them all together and freshen the conversation when it lapses. And, as I recall, their son is just about your age. Pay him some special attention, will you, honey? He's a nice boy."

Georgia snatched her phone out of her purse and flipped some more pages in her party planner, until she found the address-book section.

Time for plan B. She was older and wiser in the ways of the world now. She would simply see to it that some nice girl was invited to amuse Cootie for some preparty festivities. If she were successful, she could forget him and focus on Brandon. A French-tipped nail at the end of her slender finger finally landed on the perfect specimen.

"Boatright," Georgia murmured. Matilda. Or Bunny Boatright, as she was known, due to the pronounced protrusion of her front teeth and the rather unfortunate size of her ears. She hailed from up near Paddock Rock but could no doubt be summoned for dinner if she thought an eligible bachelor would be there to play her dinner companion.

As she waited for Bunny to pick up, Georgia blew past a slow-moving tractor-trailer rig at slightly over a hundred miles per hour. This Bunny thing had to work. They were perfect for each other. A few moments spent here and there to pique their interest in each other, and Georgia could concentrate on Brandon. Already Georgia was beginning to feel much better.

That is, until she saw the red and blue lights flashing in her rearview mirror.

Five hundred dollars, a black mark on her driving record and twenty minutes later, Georgia arrived at the Circle BO in a worse mood, if possible, than when she'd left Brandon's place. At least Bunny had been patient with her on the phone and agreed to a little gathering here at the ranch tonight.

As Georgia pulled into her personal parking space, she could see the signs of the first guests beginning to arrive and settle into their various suites. Some were to be hosted inside the enormous wings of the mansion and some in palatial guest houses, situated in various scenic woodland groupings beyond the white-fenced horse pastures.

As he enthusiastically directed the sweating legions of subcontractors, her diminutive uncle, Big Daddy Brubaker, was already reveling in the party atmosphere. Georgia couldn't help but smile. He was such a little darling. Tents were being erected, roasting pits dug and outdoor lights wired. Band members and their roadies unloaded into the special amphitheater built just for this occasion, and servants bustled to and fro, ferrying guests in special golf carts. It was already a madhouse and the party wasn't even scheduled to begin until day after tomorrow.

From what Miss Clarise had indicated on the phone, the Biggles-Vanderhousen family was now taking refreshments in the front parlor, bottom floor of the Dallas/Ft. Worth wing. As she trotted down the echoing hallway,

Georgia could only hope that Carter had gone from the ugly duckling to a swan.

The moment she entered the room, Georgia's eyes sought and found little Cootie. Or at least the back of his head. He was sitting alone in a love seat, across from his parents, who were both seated in matching side-by-side club chairs. She immediately recognized his parents, even though they'd gone from jet-black hair to silver and had both put on weight.

As Georgia moved further into the room and toward the small grouping, she could better see Carter Biggles-Vanderhousen and noticed, with a swift intake of breath, that he had gone from an ugly duckling to...an ugly duck.

It was incredible.

Though she hadn't expected miracles, she had imagined that he would have at least learned to follow the trends of fashion. Or even color-coordinate his clothing. Or simply sit up straight. But he hadn't changed a single bit. He was simply a *larger* version of the same old goofy Cootie. His baggy clothes were rumpled, as was his less-than-stylish hair. He had several days' whisker growth on his chin, and Georgia couldn't really tell if he was trying to grow a beard or he'd simply forgotten to shave. His horrible glasses were thick, and in this light he looked rather sallow. There were dark circles under his eyes, as if he hadn't slept in days.

Weeks, maybe.

And yet Miss Clarise didn't seem at all fazed by his appearance as she reintroduced her niece to Carter B. Vanderhousen.

"Georgia, darlin'! At last! You're heah! Look, Carter. It's Georgia. Isn't she a beauty? And, Georgia, isn't it fabulous to have our brilliant Carter back? I just know you two will have such a grand time reminissin'."

Really, Georgia mused, Miss Clarise should win some kind of award for social grace and diplomacy. The genteel woman treated the vacantly staring man as if he were some sort of wunderkind royalty, her enthusiasm for him not one whit diminished by his lack of response.

"You two used to be tighter than my granny's corset." Miss Clarise's face was an animated pink and her usually soft drawl buoyant. "Why it seems as if just yesterday, these two were huntin' grasshoppahs down by the creek. Remember that, Daisy?"

Carter's mother beamed at the memory and reached over to pat her son's wrinkled khaki thigh. "Oh, weren't they adorable? Carter was always bringin' home some creature in his pockets. Though, I had to draw the line at venom. I never could scold him, though. He was just too cute."

Georgia gaped at the woman. Then—at Miss Clarise's beckoning—she remembered her manners and sidled up to her aunt where she hovered awkwardly at the older woman's elbow. She forced her lips to curve over her grinding molars. *Cute?* Was the woman daft? Cootie had been anything but cute back then, and unfortunately, time had not helped in this matter. Avoiding his weird, otherworldly gaze, Georgia sidled closer to the arm of her aunt's chair.

"And now," Carter's mother said, beaming, "we are just so proud of him, and glad of this opportunity to brag on him and show him off to our old friends and such. You know how it is, Miss Clarise."

"Oh, yes, indeed I do." The hostess reached behind her shoulder and took Georgia's hand in her own. "We are absurdly proud of our youngsters."

"How are your parents?" Harlan Biggles-Vanderhousen, Carter's father, inquired of Georgia.

"Very well, thank you." Georgia's eyes strayed to Cootie for a horrible split second. He was staring. Not at her. Through her. "They, uh," she tried to focus on what she was saying even as she was being X-rayed, "they will arrive in a day or two, for the actual beginning of the party."

Daisy hooted. "We couldn't wait that long, could we Harlan? We just never could stay away from our friends at the Circle BO."

No. Georgia had to agree. Nor could they seem to leave their son behind. Even at the ripe old age of…she did some mental calculating, twenty-five, Carter was clearly still a mama's boy. Hangin' out with mommy and daddy. And she thought *she* was a loser.

"Georgia, darlin', you remember all the good times with Carter?" Miss Clarise gestured for her niece to take a seat next to Carter on the suddenly far too tiny love seat.

"I…why, I…why…who could forget? Hello, Carter," she chirped as she gingerly perched on the cushion next to his.

"Hi." His vacant gaze swept over her knees, up her arm and came to rest in a most disconcerting fashion at her throat.

Goodness. Georgia's hand rose to shield her neck. Any minute now he'd certainly sprout bat's wings and fly out the window to his secret lair. She shivered. With a quart or two of her blood, no doubt.

"Hi." Voice hoarse, she clutched the arm of the love seat with her free hand until her knuckles cracked.

An awkward silence filled the room for a beat until Miss Clarise launched a Q&A session on Carter's many and varied accomplishments over the past years. His parents were only too glad to fill in all the missing details, beginning back at his high school graduation, where he was named valedictorian and salutatorian, and all-around science wizard.

Georgia promptly tuned out the bragfest. In her peripheral vision, she could see Carter's vacant gaze float from her neck to the window and beyond.

*Hi. Huh.* She blew a tiny, silent puff of exasperation through her nose. Was that the extent of the boy genius's conversation? Was she the only person in the room who could see him for the vampire he was? A vampire with no social skills, at that.

Without really looking, Georgia watched Carter zoning out, entering his little weirdo world, clearly oblivious to the conversation that sang his praises. Oblivious to the fact he was on vacation with his parents. Oblivious to the fact that he was being reunited with the girl who'd saved him from ridicule and bullies so many times in the past. Oblivious to the fact that he was a complete freak of nature.

Was this pod guy for real?

Completely creeped out, she felt gooseflesh roar up and down her arms, and in the interest of maintaining her composure, she switched her focus back to Miss Clarise who was winding up the conversation Georgia had completely missed and was preparing to send her guests to their adjoining suites.

"Y'all will want to retire to your rooms to ready up for suppah, which will be served out on the terrace this evening for the early birds arriving for our party. There will be a lovely gathering of oilmen and other folks this evenin', perhaps five or six hundred, many of them as young as you, Carter, darlin'. Be sure to wear your dancing shoes—"

Georgia rolled her eyes in disbelief. Miss Clarise actually thought this zombie would dance? Did vampires do that stuff? Certainly, she'd stepped into an episode of *The Twilight Zone.*

"—as we have some live entertainment and a dance

floor prepared especially in honor of this special evenin' with our oldest and dearest friends."

Harlan and Daisy beamed with anticipation.

Carter maintained his faultless "bump on a log" routine.

After several torturous moments spent ushering the Biggles-Vanderhousens out of the Dallas/Ft. Worth parlor and to the main staircase, Georgia rushed around them to her room and called Brandon.

"Honey, I'm so sorry, but there is no way I'm going to be able to make our private dinner-for-two tonight. Oh, Brandon, please come over here quick and save me!"

"Save you? How?"

"Get over here right away and have dinner. And stay for dancing!"

"I'm on my way," Brandon promised, in his deep, soothing and, what was most important, *normal* voice. "Give me a half hour."

That's what she loved about Brandon. He didn't waste time with pointless questions. He simply complied.

Georgia heaved a huge sigh of relief. "Oh, Brandon, thank you! Miss Clarise pulled me aside just now and made a point of asking me to escort Carter Biggles-Vanderhousen to dinner and assist him in mingling. Honey, this guy is too *strange* for words. I can't carry the conversational ball with a zombie for two hours! Help!"

"You can count on me," Brandon assured her.

Georgia's eyes slid closed as she hung up the phone. Yes, she thought with satisfaction. She could always count on Brandon.

# Chapter Two

Georgia felt as if her smile was screwed on so tightly, it would take a plastic surgeon's knife to put her face back to normal. This little blind date she'd stirred up for Carter and Bunny Boatright was hitting the wall. Hard. And not due to lack of effort on her part. Try as she might to draw them out, Cootie was lost in a world of his own making. His only concession to "dressing up" had been to add a crooked bow tie to his travel-weary ensemble, completing his absentminded Poindexter look. Next to him, Bunny was doing her best to blend in with the broccoli on her plate.

At every other table scattered about the sprawling verandah, the guests were lively, laughing, chattering—even somewhat rambunctious—as they reminisced and enjoyed the sunset by candlelight. The antebellum mansion's patio extended beyond the glass conservatory and was embraced by an ornate concrete railing and balustrades. An enormous staircase led from the verandah proper to the rolling lawn and gardens beyond.

Melodic crickets' song underscored the tinkling of silver against china, and a warm breeze had the flames in the centerpieces flickering. On the horizon, the very first stars were beginning to twinkle, and the full moon had risen above the billowing seas of wheat.

It was a perfect evening for a small dinner party with hundreds of the family's friends and business acquaintances. The atmosphere was casual yet elegant, encouraging folks to catch up with each other over dessert, drinks or a dance on the parquet floor situated at one side of the small samba band. Other groups mingled in verandah corners, or in seating arrangements in the conservatory, or at bars located at the far ends of the dining area. The entire affair was typical Brubaker: good food, good drink, good atmosphere and good conversation.

At least at every other table.

Georgia and Brandon shared a round table with Carter and Bunny and another couple she'd never met before from Ft. Worth. Newlyweds. Deidra and Lance Covington. Seemed they only had eyes for each other. And hands. And lips.

So conversation at their table, when there had been any at all, was stilted. Awkward. Horrible. Desperately, Georgia searched her brain for some topic that would involve everyone. She smoothed the white linen tablecloth with her fingertips and dove once more into the sucking vortex that was tonight's assignment.

"Bunny!" The cords of her throat were bulging with her efforts to exude good cheer and at the same time drag more than one-word sentences from these social clods. "I know you must remember Carter from grade school. He comes from a long line of oilmen. Why, the Big V is one of the states biggest producers, right Carter?"

Carter nodded.

"And, Bunny, did you know that when Carter isn't busy helping his daddy run the oil world, he also owns a…a…a…uh, some kind of computer business?"

"No," Bunny murmured to her cauliflower.

"Well, he does, and according to his mama, he's a regular guru. Right, Carter?"

"Wrong."

Dang. She should have paid better attention to what his parents had said about Carter's boring escapades since grade school. She was sure, however, that she'd heard the word *computer* bandied about. Certainly he worked with computers. Didn't everybody these days? Especially human moles like Carter. She'd have to try another angle to draw him out. "Surely, Carter, you're just being too hard on yourself."

"No."

"You are not being too hard on yourself?"

"No."

Georgia glanced around the table, her perky expression fading as her gaze landed on Brandon. She was sure the sparks from her eyes telegraphed her exasperation. Swallowing her ire, she chirped, "No, as in, I'm wrong?"

"Wrong."

"What—" Georgia sighed and turned to Bunny "—ever. Scratch that computer thing." To Carter she said, "Why don't you tell us exactly what you do for a living?"

"No."

"Why not?"

"You wouldn't be interested."

He had *that* right. Still, if you couldn't talk about what

you did for a living to kick-start the get-acquainted chit-chat, what other topics were there?

Georgia exchanged yet another droll glance with Brandon, then peeked at her watch. Criminy sakes, they'd only been sitting here for fifteen minutes. And yet, it seemed a lifetime. She was dying to grab Brandon and bolt. However, for Miss Clarise's sake, she sallied forth, vowing to get Carter and Bunny together if it killed her.

"Ooo. I think you're using reverse psychology, huh? Trying to play the mystery man, you rascal." Even to Georgia's own ears, her phony laughter sounded like an ass's bray.

Carter simply stared at her.

Feeling foolish but also angry enough to be beyond caring, Georgia forged ahead. "Hmm. Whatever it is he does for a living must be very…*interesting*. Right, Bunny? Bunny loves interesting career stories, don't you, hon?"

Bunny blushed and shrugged around a mouthful of carrots. "Mmm."

"Bunny is single, too, Carter. You two have a lot in common, being single and having such interesting careers." Both were dowdy, crashing bores. Perfect for each other. "Bunny volunteers for a charity children's dentist, booking appointments. You have to use a computer there, right Bunny? I'll bet you have some questions for Carter about that, huh, Bunny?"

"Uh, well, I guess…really, no."

"Okay, Carter, you must visit the dentist now and then, right? I bet you and Bunny have a ton in common about that, huh?"

"No."

"No, you don't visit the dentist, or no, you don't have any teeth?" Georgia hated the sarcasm that tinged her words, but hang it all, this conversation was worse than a root canal.

A very slight smile tinged his lips.

Her tone grim, she barked, "Why don't you just put us out of our misery and tell us what it is that you *do* do, Carter?"

Heads jerked up all around and everyone bit back smiles.

"Why?"

"Why not? Is it—" she glanced around the table with a smirk "—top secret?"

"Yeah. Right." His nod was amiable enough.

Okay. There was another dead end. She clutched Brandon's knee and squeezed a help-me-out-here message. Ever faithful, he reached under the table and gave her hand a reassuring pat.

"Well, that's nice." Brandon issued a jovial chuckle. "Now that we have the career thing sorted out, why don't we move on to politics or religion?"

Nobody laughed.

"How about those Yankees?"

Again, no response.

Radiating exasperation despite her spunky smile, Georgia pushed her chair back and clutched her purse. "All righty. On that note, I feel the need to…freshen up. Please, continue visiting amongst yourselves. I'll return in a moment."

"Do you want me to come with you?" Brandon whispered.

Bless his heart. So trustworthy. So predictable. She patted his shoulder. "No, hon." She dipped and whispered, "Ladies' room."

"Ah." Brandon nodded and dropped back into his seat.

With that, she made good her escape.

Upon entering the ladies' lounge, Georgia dumped her purse and picked out two ibuprofen tablets and tossed them down her throat and chased them with water in a paper cup.

As she removed her makeup case and peered into the mirror, she could hear several men who had bellied up to a small bar—just outside the ladies' room lounge—and were holding a rather…vigorous conversation.

With great care Georgia reapplied her lipstick, wanting her lips to look tantalizing for Brandon and any public displays he might be up for this evening. Not that she felt they were ready for that. Yet. But after this dreary dinner party, at least she could tackle the project in a more serious frame of mind, slurps and all.

She didn't start out to eavesdrop, but as the men's discussion grew heated, she paused, her lips pressed together to even the color. By the sound of things, it was just some good ol' boy types who'd had a tad too much to drink and were feeling their oats. Safe among the oil brotherhood, they spoke freely, if not somewhat drunkenly. Georgia rolled her eyes. All her life she'd been subjected to the endlessly boring subject of petroleum and its position in the current market place. She stifled a yawn.

Then she grew still.

The suppressed fury in one man's low voice caught her attention and she leaned toward the door to hear better.

"We can't have this maggot eating our livelihood out from under us. If he succeeds in mass marketing this 'alternative' fuel, we'll eventually be out of business."

A calmer man whom some of the guys were calling Flint said, "You'll eventually be out of business anyway, Rocky. Petroleum is not a renewable resource, unless we can start us up a dinosaur herd."

The group laughed.

Rocky, on the other hand, didn't see the humor and swore through a tight jaw. "We got *years* before we run out of oil. I don't want to be put out of business until we have to."

Lipstick dangling in her hand, Georgia frowned. What on earth could he be so up in arms about? Wasn't everything just fine in the oil world? Big Daddy certainly seemed carefree enough this evening. She snapped her lipstick closed and swiped her cosmetics over the edge of the counter and into her clutch. Moving to the lounge's door, she pretended to adjust her hair in the full-length mirror as she strained to catch a bit more of the dirt. At least *this* conversation was animated. Sure beat returning to the bores at her table.

Amid their complaints, the major source of discontent seemed to be over some successful new upstart company, run by a—Georgia bit back an amused smile—"phantom," who it seemed was attempting to put the petrol industry out of business with his newfangled alternative to oil fuel.

"As if wind would ever replace gas," one man snorted.

"Or water and solar power," another chimed in.

They shared some nervous laughter over these subjects. Flint, the seeming voice of reason, said, "I don't think we have that much to worry about."

Rocky, sounding a tad further along in his drinking, disagreed again. "It's not about that stuff. This guy has come up with an energy source that mimics perpetual motion. If he succeeds, and the price is right, he could put us all out of business in a heartbeat. The oil business on a global level would dry up."

"I don't believe it."

"Believe it. Before television, idiots like you said that sending pictures over the air couldn't be done. Same with flying. And putting men on the moon. Same with this."

There was a worried silence. Georgia frowned.

"Where's he from?"

"Who knows. We don't know anything. Just rumors.

Speculation. And a few clues. Hearsay is he travels all over the world. But he had to have some experience in the business. We might know him." Rocky squinted around. "In fact, he might just be one of you."

"Bull." Flint laughed nervously. "No oilman would ever launch such a stupid enterprise against the hand that feeds him and his family. And his neighbors. Not and live to tell the tale."

Similar opinions were expressed by everyone. Then, to show their solidarity, they began to boast about what they would do to this phantom guy, if they ever got ahold of him. There was some joking about an old-fashioned tar-and-feathering and other crazy notions, but a couple of them began to get serious. Angry. Rocky's mob mentality was contagious.

The tiny hairs at the back of Georgia's neck stood up. Clearly these guys were getting a little carried away. Uncomfortable with the direction of the conversation, Georgia slipped from where she'd been hovering in the ladies' lounge and moved to the punch table to get a better look at who'd been talking. Covertly she took a moment to check them out.

Oh, yeah.

She'd seen some of them around, at fund-raisers and Oilmen's Association meetings hosted here at the Circle BO in the past. What did these yahoos mean about some silly phantom destroying the oil business? That could never happen, could it?

No.

Cheeks puffed, she exhaled her anxiety and had to laugh. Why, they sounded like something straight out of a movie. They were just complaining, that's all. Riled up. Drunk. It was all just a tempest in a beer stein. Typical

mountain/molehill stuff. Brother. If they hated their jobs
so much, why didn't they simply sell out? Giving her head
a tiny shake, she decided it was time to get back and face
the oddballs at her own table.

As she pushed off from the doorway she'd been leaning against, she could see Rocky's gaze narrow and latch
on to her as she passed. A chill skittered down her spine at
the unbridled fury she saw flashing in his eyes. Had he seen
that she'd been eavesdropping? Twin patches of heat colored her cheeks. Uh-oh.

Caught red-handed. How mortifying. She stumbled over
the hem of her skirt. With a smile of apology and a nod,
Georgia scurried back to her table, where, though she
might be bored to death, at least there was no danger of
being dipped in tar.

Darling Brandon played her besotted lover to a T. But
to what end? Old Cootie didn't even seem to get the message that she was far too deeply involved in a meaningful
relationship to devote her week to playing his personal
hostess. Nor did he seem the least bit interested in striking
up a friendship with poor Bunny Boatright.

Georgia suppressed a weary groan. Would she have to
be responsible for dragging this turtle out of his shell all
week long? Grade school all over again. She rubbed her
throbbing brow.

As dessert was served, the band began to play and Miss
Clarise paused in her mingling as she passed their table.

"Hello, children. I'm so glad to see y'all renewin' your
old friendships and makin' new ones. Isn't the night glo-
rious? I see the newlywed Covingtons are out cuttin' a rug
already. Georgia, darlin', why don't you take our Carter for
a little spin out on the dance floor. You'd like that, wouldn't

you, Carter? And, Brandon, perhaps you might ask Bunny if she's inclined to samba." Their senior hostess stood, smiling at the foursome, waiting for someone to make the first move.

"Oh…I…we…it's…" Georgia racked her brain for an excuse to get out of dancing. "Actually…I…we…"

"All right," Carter said without ceremony. Drawing his lanky body to a full standing posture, he held his hand out to Georgia. "Join me?"

"Oh…I…we…it's…"

"Go on, darlin'," Miss Clarise urged. "Have fun." She twittered and moved on to the next table.

Georgia had no choice but to comply and reach for Carter's hand. She didn't know what she'd anticipated, but his grip was surprisingly firm. His hands were large, nicely shaped and warm. Not at all the clammy dough balls she'd expected.

"Bunny?" Brandon shrugged and extended his hand to the retiring—and mortified—socialite. "Dance?"

"Okay," Bunny murmured into her crème brûlée, her face flaming. Without looking up, she flopped a limp hand in Brandon's direction and shuffled after him.

The band was wonderful and the dance floor alive and hopping. With complete confidence, Carter marched into the center of the floor and yanked Georgia into his arms. Quite suddenly—and much to her eternal amazement—she found herself in the eye of a samba tornado and being put through some pretty complex paces by little Cootie Biggles.

*Wow.* Like a lightning bolt, shock rocketed through Georgia.

He was no longer trampling her toes. In fact—giddy bubbles of amazement crowded into her throat as he whirled her out away from his body and then firmly back—

he was *fabulous*. Practically professional. Never before had she danced with such a self-assured partner. It was almost as if he could read her mind and she, his. Hair flying, skirt twirling, feet skipping on air, Georgia found herself laughing with a carefree abandon she hadn't felt in years. Her heart in her throat, Georgia held on tightly to Carter as they moved in perfect sync to the driving beat.

What an *anomaly*.

Who'd ever have believed it? Little Cootie Biggles could *dance*. Oh, baby, baby, could he *ever*. He led her with such confidence and precision, Georgia had to wonder what other curious talents lay hidden under those baggy clothes.

After several minutes of feeling as though she'd been riding a roller coaster over thunderclouds, the music slowed and Carter deftly pulled her into his arms. Delirious bubbles were still rising from her stomach to her throat and without stopping to overanalyze, Georgia leaned back and grinned up at Carter. And amazingly he returned her grin, revealing a set of perfect pearly whites.

"Ah. So you do have teeth."

"Yep."

"You ever use more than one word at a time?"

"Sometimes."

Again Georgia laughed, and Carter easily matched the pace of their feet to match the beat of the music. As naturally as if she'd been dancing with him all her life—which, she guessed if she counted their parents' day pageant stint in grade school, they had—Georgia settled into his arms and laid her cheek against his chest and her hand at the small of his back.

Interesting.

Under these outlandish big-and-tall togs, there was a

pretty steely frame. Curiosity piqued, she allowed her hand to do some covert roving from the sturdy narrow vee of his lower back to the wider planes just beneath his shoulder blades.

To say she was surprised would be a gross understatement. She'd expected skin and bones, but as far as she could tell, there was quite a bit of muscle under there. Exactly how *much* muscle was debatable, as any more groping at this point would seem a bit suspect. Still, he was hardly the puny, sickly character of yesteryear. Strange, as Carter didn't strike her as one who spent much time in the gym. Then again, he didn't strike her as a world-class samba dancer, either, but there she was.

She stole a peek at his face.

He looked the same. As scruffy and rumpled as an unmade bed. Even so, something about him was different. Not necessarily appealing, but different certainly from the klutzy kid he'd been. Georgia allowed her bold gaze to move up into his hugely magnified eyes.

Deep, brown eyes the color of aged whiskey. Exaggerated the way they were, she could see tiny reflective flecks, like the flashes of fireflies scattered in a night sky. And his lashes. Good grief. Sooty, thick, long, completely unfair on a man. She had to spend hours with a mascara wand to create such a natural effect. Why had she never noticed his eyes before? Probably because they were always hidden behind a ridiculous, out-of-fashion pair of glasses.

He arched a lazy brow and she squinted. In a very weird way, she found his abilities on the dance floor charming. And absurdly…sexy.

"Where did you learn to dance?"

"Latin America."

"Yeah. Right." Her eyes narrowed. When had Cootie

gotten out of the computer lab and into Latin America? And who would he dance with? Why would someone like him ever be interested in dancing? He was truly an enigma. "You're kidding."

"No."

There he went, with the one-word answers. "What were you doing in Latin America?"

"Working."

"And you took dance lessons?"

"Mmm-hmm."

"Why?"

"Because I wanted to impress a woman."

Skeptical, Georgia cocked her head. *What?* There actually lurked a human heart beneath the robotic facade? Curious, she demanded that he elaborate on his life since she saw him last. "And use more than one word at a time."

And so, as he complied with her wishes, a veritable 007-type lifestyle began to emerge. He told her of his schooling both here and abroad where he studied chemistry and biotechnology. From there, he recounted many of his incredible adventures working with the Peace Corps, near-death experiences with both dysentery and the business end of a terrorist's rifle, living in jungles, working for a company whose groundbreaking inventions were… "top secret." There was a trace of mockery in his smile as he tossed her own term for his career back in her face.

Slowly she closed her sagging jaw.

He was pulling her leg. He'd made all this up because he was paying her back for her rather high-handed attitude toward him at dinner. And for some ridiculous reason, that hurt her feelings just the tiniest bit.

She should have known from the minute he opened his mouth that he was joshing her, but she'd become completely entranced by the pictures he painted. How gullible could she be? She gave her head a tiny shake and snorted. A socially backward brain boy like him would never lead such a life of intrigue.

The very idea was ludicrous.

The quest for adventure, traveling to foreign countries, dramatic rescues, inventions, time spent in a Middle Eastern prison, being tortured for information, spies and bad guys, and now living his life…how did he phrase it? Oh yes, "below the radar." What a bunch of hooey.

Well, in any event, he was either playing her for a fool, or he led a very rich fantasy life. Really. She oughta send him over to gab with the drunks outside the ladies' lounge. They were all delusional.

Big Daddy sure had some unusual characters in his social circle.

She sighed.

Still, at the very least Carter's crazy stories beat prying conversation from him one word at a time. On him, this comic-book-hero thing, though ridiculous, was entertaining, especially considering she had to dance with him.

So, since she had little else to do at the moment, Georgia feigned ignorance to his game and goaded him on. And as he spoke, she was surprised to find herself getting lost once more in his crazy tales the way she would a scene straight out of *Dr. No* or *Goldfinger.* He was a pretty talented storyteller.

Eventually she led the subject full circle and back to his fantasy about the Latin American woman.

"Have you ever had a serious love affair?" Georgia awaited his answer with subdued skepticism, knowing he'd probably invent a harem of some kind, solely for her benefit.

"You mean like you and…Brandon?" Large, mocha-java eyes peered deeply into hers, and Georgia suddenly felt defensive.

"I guess." She sniffed.

"I find that I attract a different breed of women than the easily bruised Southern peaches I grew up around."

"Probably because the way you dress attracts different…breeds."

"Ah. Humor." Carter's smile was benign as he effectively cut off any further conversation by drawing her back against his chest.

She rolled her eyes and scanned the terrace for Brandon. Like an obedient dog, he was standing at the edge of the dance floor, patiently waiting for her to signal his next move.

Mistaking her eye contact as a plea for help, Brandon cut in on Georgia and Carter, ever dutiful and aware that she had asked him to stick by her side. Georgia thought she saw the tiniest spark of disappointment flash behind Carter's chunky lenses as he turned her over to Brandon, but then, Georgia couldn't be certain if it was a real emotion or simply the glare from the candlelight. No matter.

She was finally free to enjoy a dance with Brandon.

"I'm sorry, honey. Have you been bored?"

Brandon shrugged. "I had a nice dance with Bunny. She's not so bad, one-on-one. In fact—"

"Brandon?" Georgia watched Carter saunter over to Bunny and ask for a dance. A most insane shard of jealousy pierced her soul for a split second. Bunny would never be able to follow Carter's lead. Not the way she had. Why, they'd been as fluid as a glass of water, the two of them. She gave her head a tiny shake to clear her idiotic need to constantly compete. "Brandon…"

"Hmm?" Brandon murmured into her hair.

"What do you know about alternative fuel?"

Her curiosity had been aroused by the debate still raging at the bar outside the ladies' lounge.

"Which kind specifically? There are a growing number of choices ranging from wind and wood to ethanol created by corn."

"The perpetual-motion kind."

Brandon chuckled. "There is no such thing."

"What if there was such a thing? Why wouldn't oilmen like the idea? After all, oil can't last forever. Wouldn't they be interested in funding research?"

"What?" Brandon lifted an amused brow. "Fund research that would put our industry out of business? Where would you come up with an idea like that?"

"Don't look now, but I heard some men over by the ladies' room—" Georgia smacked his arm "—Brandon! I said don't look! Did they see you?"

Brandon waved at the men. "Yeah, so?"

"Promise you won't look again, and I'll tell you."

Brandon chuckled. "Go on."

"Okay. I was in the lounge, and those men were having this really bizarre conversation about this person they call the phantom—"

"The *phantom?*" Brandon rolled his eyes and again glanced over at Rocky and his cronies. "Ooo, sounds like somebody's been watching too many scary movies—"

"Shh! Would you please stop gawking and listen? They said this phantom had invented some kind of perpetual-motion thing, and they sounded like they wanted to kill him."

"Well…actually that's not exactly outside the realm of possibility." Brandon's laughter was casual considering the topic. "But not from them. Those guys are just second-rate hackers, talking big. But there are a lot of powerful men in the industry who aren't what you'd call 'big on change.' And some people like them have a bit of a mob mentality. They protect what's theirs. At all costs. Remember, Georgia, there is *huge* money in oil. And wherever you have big money, you have big criminals. The oil world is no different."

"Yes," she agreed, "but only for the time being. Someday oil will run out, right?"

"Yes, but not before these people are long gone."

"Oh." Georgia frowned. "Then why all the hubbub?"

"Because these days nothing is certain in our world politics. And that scares people. But—" Brandon cupped her chin with his hand and tilted her face up to his "—I'll tell you one thing that is certain…"

"What?"

"You're beautiful tonight."

Georgia colored and glanced over at Carter who was dragging a lifeless Bunny around the dance floor.

Brandon's voice was velvety low in her ear. "You know, I couldn't stop thinking about that kiss we shared this afternoon."

"Really?" Guiltily Georgia glanced down at her shoes. She hadn't thought of it once.

"Mmm." Brandon held her close, swaying to the music. "There will be more where that came from, later," he promised.

"Okay." Georgia sighed. Relaxing against his broad chest, she watched Cootie and Bunny struggle to find their rhythm. A glance at the clock told her that the night was young, but oddly she felt as if she'd been here for hours.

The musicians eventually took a break, and after another round of punch, Georgia needed to excuse herself from

Brandon for a trip to the powder room. The conversation among the oilmen still raged at the nearby bar and had even intensified.

Flint was talking as she slipped by. "Yeah, yeah, yeah, Rocky. We hear your point, but it's a free country, and the phantom is not doing anything against the law."

Rocky was well lubricated now and slurring with righteous indignation. "Oh, yeah? Maybe. But putting me out of business is against *my* law."

Several other oilmen chimed in, agreeing with Rocky.

"Listen…" Spittle flying, Rocky pounded his fist on the bar. "I have a smaller operation. Already the mergers of the bigger companies have hurt me bad. Take just a small percentage of my customers and convince them that this mystery fuel crap is the less expensive, more dependable and cleaner wave of the future, and I'm dead in the water. *Dead!*"

Unable to resist a peek, Georgia slipped out the door to the ladies' room and hovered behind a ficus plant. She watched in morbid fascination as Rocky downed his entire drink in one swallow and came up outraged. His body language radiated fury and his eyes were wild. "I say we do it. I have connections. I know how to get the job done."

Flint cast a nervous glanced around, then cautioned him to lower his voice. "Not again, Rocky."

Rocky clutched the bar top. "And what's he doing to us? *Killing* us! That's what! Taking the food out of our mouths. I won't stand for it. Neither should you."

"You need to cool down, buddy. We know you're just talkin'," one of the more levelheaded men told him.

"I think he means it," another said. "You know he's set up to butcher his livestock with a mobile unit. Clean, simple, no fuss, no muss. Right, Rocky?"

Thoroughly chilled at their sinister tone, Georgia felt Rocky suddenly notice her and focus his bloodshot eyes through the branches of the tiny tree where she stood.

# *Chapter Three*

As Carter herded the docile Bunny Boatright around the dance floor, he found it virtually impossible to keep his attention on the task at hand. Not that Bunny was a bad dancer, exactly. She was simply…flaccid. Dancing with her was like dancing with yesterday's Caesar salad. Wilted, somewhat soggy and vastly unappealing. Even so, Bunny could have been Ginger Rogers herself and Carter wouldn't have noticed.

Not when Georgia Brubaker was in the room.

From the moment he'd set eyes on her earlier that afternoon, all the feelings he'd worked so hard to bury over the years had come flooding back. And this time they carried the intensity of a full-blown animal attraction of a man for a woman. He hated such weakness in himself. From the moment he'd heard about this party, he'd worked hard at steeling himself against any kind of emotional reaction. He'd even gone out of his way to show that he was impervious to Georgia by dressing down and bowing out of the conversation. In fact, the only reason he'd agreed to attend this shindig in the first place was to prove that after all this time he was over his ridiculous—and completely futile—fascination with Georgia.

But no.

If anything, his feelings for her had returned with a vengeance, rendering him a vegetable at the first sight of her.

He spun the noodle-like Bunny around so that he could observe as Georgia stepped out from where—for some strange reason—she'd been hovering behind a plant. Carter frowned. She approached some drunken, and clearly leering, oilmen and made polite small talk. Why would she do a thing like that? Of course, he realized she was simply playing the hostess, but these idiots were fairly drooling. His hands clenched, causing Bunny to squeak.

"Sorry," he muttered.

Though she smiled, Bunny's enormous teeth seemed to point at him in accusation, and Carter, guilt-ridden, knew he hadn't been paying proper attention. But hang it all. It wasn't as if Bunny and he had any kind of future together. At this point in his career, Carter had no time for a relationship. With anyone. Period. Let alone the terminally shy Miss Boatright. Ignoring Bunny's fiery blush, Carter aggressively danced her through the crowd and closer to Georgia for a better look. Then, putting his dance moves on autopilot, he hovered at the edge of the parquet floor and strained to see through the shadows.

Why was he doing this? Following Georgia around like some kind of lovesick puppy. Because he was an idiot. A besotted idiot. With bad hair and clothes. Just like preschool.

Hot tingles flashed up one side of his body and sailed down the other as Georgia came into his line of focus.

Lord, have mercy. Standing there in the flickering candle-light, she was even more spectacular than ever. As though parched after a long stint in the desert, Carter allowed his eyes to drink in every detail of the changes that had occurred since he'd seen her last.

Her dress was a study in simplicity and was no doubt tailor-made just for this occasion. It fitted her like a silky second skin, flowing over her curvy body and swirling about her ankles with every step. He attempted to swallow. The image of her hip beneath his hand back on the dance floor had his mouth going dry all over again.

As he'd always imagined, she'd been a dream partner. Light and lithe she had followed his every move with skill. Joy. Passion. And though he knew she disdained him, he could tell that she felt their extraordinary connection as they danced. A tiny grin tugged at the corner of his mouth. Surprise. Little Cootie could stay on his feet.

His gaze drifted to her satiny, straight and streaky blond hair, and he briefly wondered if it felt as soft and thick as it looked, before his eyes dipped to take in the rest of her features. Dimples bloomed whenever she smiled, and she was nearly always smiling and full of endlessly perky chatter. She reminded him of a famous morning talk-show hostess he liked. Georgia would have been good at a job like that. She was seductive that way. Able to draw a person out, even when they didn't want to converse.

In fact—Carter pulled the inside of his lower lip between his teeth and gnawed—he'd talked way too much with her on the dance floor. Very unusual for him.

He'd learned early on in life to keep his thoughts to himself or suffer the ridicule later. But Georgia had a way of making his lips loose. Ever since he was a little kid, he'd felt unnaturally safe sharing his dreams and fantasies with her. Even so, he should have known better than to blather on the way he had.

But she'd goaded him.

And for once in his adult life, his need to impress had overridden his common sense. No doubt now she saw him as a bigger fool than ever. Carter snorted. Didn't really matter. That was nothing new. Luckily she hadn't believed a word he'd said.

Finally Carter stopped pretending to dance altogether and simply swayed Bunny to and fro. Georgia continued to chat away with the inebriated wolf pack as though they were visiting dignitaries. One of them was clearly on the prowl. Standing a little too close, talking a little too loud, staring a little too hard.

He could feel his blood pressure rise.

She was still smiling, but now…now she seemed a tad stiff. There was agitation in her manner. He tensed. Were they hassling her? Too late, he dropped Bunny's hand and moved to rescue Georgia only to find himself beaten to the punch by Brandon McGraw.

He took a step back and sighed.

Good old quickdraw McGraw.

What did she see in that foppish dandy?

A rueful smile twisted his lips. A helluva lot more than she'd ever seen in him, he reckoned. Not that there was anything wrong with the foppish sort, if that's what she wanted, but this McGraw character certainly didn't suit the Georgia he remembered. She and Brandon McGraw were a terrible mismatch. Their friendship made his stomach churn.

"Are we done dancing?" Bunny wondered, her lips clinging in a puzzled purse to her prodigious front teeth.

Carter gave her a distracted nod, and without comment, Bunny faded into the shadows. Unencumbered now, he moved over to the bar and got in line, never once letting Georgia leave his sight. While he waited to be served, he strained unsuccessfully to hear what she and McGraw were chatting about with the oilmen, but the party hubbub made it impossible.

Even though her back was to him, Carter could tell Georgia was finished with the boorish conversation and was trying to back away. However, the men had engaged the sociable McGraw now, making escape politically incorrect at the moment. The muscles in Carter's jaw tensed at the look on Georgia's face. Too bad her man didn't seem to notice her discomfort. Just because she was the hostess didn't mean she had to suffer the inane blathering of a bunch of drunks. If he'd been her date, he'd have made excuses and hustled her out of there. Clearly, that's what she wanted.

He knew all too well what Georgia did and did not want.

Until they were eight, anyway.

Then she'd gone and moved with her parents from Hidden Valley to the other end of the world. Or so Oklahoma had seemed to a third-grade boy. Being a scrawny child, and a daydreamer to boot, he'd been picked on by the other kids. Teased. Bullied. Georgia had always been there to champion him at school. And church. And play group. And anywhere and everywhere he'd been foisted off on her, simply because they happened to be the same age, from the same neighborhood and the same social circle.

If she resented entertaining him, she'd never let on, making sure he was included, even when the other kids objected. She'd made him feel a part of things. And at times, even normal. He'd loved her for that. Adored her.

Worshipped at her saddle shoes.

Yep. Saying goodbye to Georgia Brubaker was the hardest thing he'd ever done in his short life, and the childish pain he'd suffered over that loss still had the power to thicken his throat. It had been a dark day, the day she rode off down the Circle BO's mile-long driveway in one of two stretch limousines. Hanging out the window, hair whipping in the wind, smiling all the way, she'd waved goodbye to her cousins and family friends and life as she'd known it since she was born.

Carter knew she'd waved for the entire mile because he'd run after her until they turned out of sight. Once they'd disappeared, breathless and dying inside, he'd retreated to Big Daddy's haymow to cry in solitude.

And he had cried.

Buckets. Cried till his eyes were swollen and his head ached. Cried till his sobs were nothing but dry, raspy heaves. Cried till he'd fallen asleep and been woken up many hours later by a policeman's blinding flashlight. His father had thrashed him soundly for worrying his mother and Miss Clarise that way, but the punishment hadn't had the desired effect.

Carter was through crying.

He'd never confessed his unrequited feelings for Georgia to another living soul, but simply suffered in silence until the pain slowly faded. As the years passed, having no one left to defend him, he'd become tough. Hardened, both physically and emotionally. As he grew, he'd retreated into a dream world of deep thought during the day and, in the afternoons, he'd found physical outlet at the gym, where he worked at putting a little muscle on his scrawny frame, for self-defense purposes.

"Yes sir?"

"Yes?" Carter gave his head a clearing shake. He'd been woolgathering.

"What would you like to drink?"

"I, uh…" Carter realized he'd finally made it to the head of the line at the bar. He glanced over at Georgia. She was looking increasingly miserable by the minute. "Nothing, thanks." He had a damsel that needed rescuing.

Georgia immediately agreed to another dance and—after a few air kisses and some hand signals for Brandon's benefit—she practically dragged a pleasantly surprised Carter out to the dance floor.

The music was mellow now, and the couples that danced moved slowly to the languid rhythm. Georgia led Carter to the middle of the floor and allowed herself to be pulled into his embrace. She sighed and, with her forehead resting against his shoulder, fell into a deep, pensive silence.

Carter let her mull, just enjoying the feel of her warm body pressed against his as they swayed in their small section of the dance floor. But after an entire song—however much he enjoyed simply holding Georgia—his curiosity got the better of him and he had to know what kept her from her usual stream of patter.

He brought his lips to her ear and murmured, "What is it?" She shivered, and without thinking twice he pulled her closer and ran his hand over her bare back to warm her skin. Such soft skin. Just as smooth and creamy as it looked. His eyes drifted shut.

Georgia lifted a shoulder. "I…" Her laughter was self-deprecating. "You're going to think I'm nuts."

"Try me."

"I don't even know where to start."

"The beginning is usually useful."

She drew in a long, deep breath and held it, then exhaled heavily. Leaning back in his embrace, she crossed her arms over her chest and sent him a look of defiance. "Okay. I feel really foolish, but what I have to say isn't one bit stranger than all that crap you shoveled about what you do for a living now."

Unable to help himself, Carter threw back his head and shouted with laughter. She was priceless. He locked his hands comfortably at the small of her back and they swayed to the music in a passable pretense at dance.

"Don't laugh." Her expression was grumpy and she wrung her hands.

He sobered. "Okay. I won't laugh. What's going on?"

"This is going to sound really, really weird."

"Spit it out already."

"Yes." Her tongue flicked over her lips. "Do you know anything about the men that were standing by that table over there?"

"What men?"

Georgia craned her head around. "Over...that's weird."

"What's weird?"

"Brandon's gone. They're all gone."

Carter rolled his eyes. Were she and Brandon connected at the hip? With all the patience he could muster, he asked, "Why would it be weird for Brandon to strike off on his own for a few minutes? It is a free country after all."

She sent him a pained expression. "I know that. But we made a promise never to leave the other alone tonight. Not for a second. He even pinkie-swore."

"Pardon?"

"Never mind. He simply promised not to leave my side."

"Must make trips to the bathroom interesting."

"That's not what I mean and you know it. Brandon is very loyal. It's not like him to wander off without telling me where he is going."

"Mom, he's a big kid now. He can make potty all by himself."

"Ha. Very funny." Georgia frowned, distracted by the sudden absence of the entire group. "Anyway, we were talking to these oilmen—"

"Drunk? Rowdy? Loud?"

"Yes!"

"I saw you talking to them. What about 'em?"

"Well, okay—" her cheeks turned a charming shade of pink and, lowering her eyes, she spoke directly into his pectorals "—they were having a very odd conversation and really, it gave me the creeps. It almost sounded like they... Okay, this is where it gets really stupid." She glanced up at him. "But here goes…they were going all berserk about the goofiest stuff like solar power and some kind of mysterious phantom, and their mobile cattle-butchering unit and—"

Carter stood stock-still and darted a quick glance around. "So. They have people here," he muttered under his breath.

"What?"

"Nothing. Go on."

"Right. Uh, well, it almost sounded like they wanted to—" she lowered her voice to a whisper "—kill someone." Her laughter was forced. "I know they were probably just talking about the latest technology in making hamburger, but…well, okay. You can call me crazy now."

"What—" his fingers tightened around her arm "—*exactly* were they saying?"

Georgia leaned back and peered through his lenses to the light that flashed in his eyes. "You believe me?"

His eyes narrowed. "Are you telling the truth?"

"As I know it, yeah."

"Then I believe you. Continue. Now."

"Okay, I was in the bathroom, putting on my lipstick and—"

"Spare me the beauty regime."

Georgia huffed. "If I'm going to remember everything, I have to tell the story my way."

A long-suffering groan sounded in his throat.

"So, like I said, I was standing in the powder room and I could hear these oilmen gabbing. At first I didn't listen to anything they said, then after a while, it started to get a little heated. This one guy they were calling Rocky was really mad. I thought he was just a little 'tuned up,' if you know what I mean, but the more I listened, the more I understood that he was beyond angry. He sounded kind of irrational."

"About solar power?"

"Yeah. Weird, huh? He was also going off on other things like that. You know, wind power, water…any kind of fuel that wasn't oil-based like corn or coal or wood or—"

Carter waved his hands in tight circles, urging her to get to the point.

"Okay, okay. They all argued about those things for a while, and finally this Rocky guy starts spouting off some wacky stuff about some kind of—" she drew air quotes "—'phantom' who was from around these parts and maybe was even here at this party tonight, but who traveled all over the world and had some kind of inside information and who was ruining the oil business as we know it now with some kind of cockamamie perpetual-motion deal, and how he, this Rocky guy, wanted to, well, it sure *sounded* like he was talking about finding and…" Nerves had her giggling, though there was fear in her eyes. She dropped her voice. "*Butchering* the phantom. That's when he saw me."

"He *saw* you?"

"Uh, yeah. I came out of the bathroom to get a better look at who all was talking and he caught me eavesdropping. Twice."

A feeling of foreboding had Carter's heart pounding. *"Twice?"*

"I was curious."

"Is that why you were hiding behind the potted palm?"

Georgia's little shrug was sheepish. "Yes?"

"And so you suspected they were talking about *murdering somebody* and you went over to talk to them…*why?*"

"Because they asked me to?"

"Oh, for the love of—" Carter took Georgia's hand and led her from the dance floor to an out-of-the-way table in the shadows. Holding out a chair, he urged her to take a seat and then, spinning a chair between his legs, he draped his arms over the back and sat down across from her. "What did they talk about with you, after Brandon joined you? Tell me as much as you can remember from the very beginning."

There was a book of matches lying on the table, and with anxious fingers, Georgia picked it up and began tearing it apart. "It seemed to me like they were here to look for trouble. Like if this phantom guy was anywhere, he'd for sure be here. And this is where it gets a little strange."

"It *gets* strange? Honey, it's already strange."

"Yes, well, for some reason, they had a lot of questions for Brandon when he came to join the conversation."

"What kind of questions?"

"The same stuff they'd been debating earlier. Questions about what he knew about alternative-fuel sources, his opinions, stuff like that." Rattled by his obvious concern, Georgia ripped off a match and gnawed at the end. "Oh, and then they had questions about his private jet and, uh, about his education, his links to the oil community and to foreign countries.... Why are you looking at me that way?"

"What were Brandon's responses?"

"Well, Brandon is very protective of me."

Carter's shoulder's dropped and he groaned. "What does *that* mean?"

"Well, he can be kind of…you know, snotty when he feels threatened, so I think he was putting them on. Having a little fun with them. You know, to get rid of them. He didn't like the way they were eyeing me."

"What do you mean when you say he was 'putting them on'?"

"He thought they were so drunk they'd never remember his answers, so he told 'em stuff to kind of make them mad, like he believed there was a growing global shift in public demand from petroleum to alternative fuel, and that very soon alternative fuel sources would be the wave of the future, which is really funny because he had just told me—"

Carter's eyes widened. "He said *that?*"

"Yeah. Why is that so bad?"

Frustrated, Carter drove his hands through his hair. "No, no. It's…it's… Go on."

"Carter, the way you're looking at me is making me really nervous."

"Sorry. Please continue."

Georgia had shredded the matchbook into a tiny pile of paper and was starting on the matches. "So, where was I? Oh, yes, Brandon was going on and on about how the world of oil was becoming obsolete and how he was diversifying into all this crazy stuff like flux capacitors and reverse vacuum energy and amalgam diode transistors and making up all these ridiculous—"

"How did they react?"

"Well, they were laughing and stuff, but they were looking at each other like, 'Is he for real?' and that Rocky guy just kept staring at me, which I think made Brandon really mad, so he started talking even crazier—"

Carter's eyes slid closed. "Crazier?"

"Well, you kind of have to know him to understand, but Brandon has this really dark, sort of dry sense of humor, and it gets really sarcastic when he's mad, you know?" Georgia stuck the match she'd been chewing into the centerpiece flame and it flared to life. "Anyway, he told them that he and I had developed this perpetual-motion thing—"

"The two of you."

"Yes."

"Developed a perpetual-motion thing."

"Yes."

Carter froze, focused on the match as it burned toward Georgia's fingertips. In a very low voice he asked, "And you say they are all gone now. Brandon and all the men he was talking to."

Georgia scanned the room. "Yes. And what's weird is that Brandon is like Old Faithful. He never just up and—"

"Oh, hell." Carter jumped to his feet so fast that Georgia dropped the smoldering match into the shredded pile of matchbook she'd made on the table. Within a fraction of a second the little pile burst into flame.

Carter stared at it for a single heartbeat, then shrugged. Perhaps it was just the diversion he needed to disappear without inviting attention. Not giving Georgia a chance to be sidetracked by something so trivial as fire, Carter pulled her to her feet and hustled her across the verandah by the wrist. Protesting all the while, she stumbled along as he tugged her to the stairs that led to the lawn and beyond.

"*Carter!* Stop! *Wait!* We can't go now, I've just set the table on *fire!*" Jaw sagging, Georgia strained to see over her shoulder while she struggled to free her wrist from Carter's cast-iron grip.

"We'll worry about that later. I have to get you out of here. Now."

"*Now?* But…but…Carter! The *fire!* I have—" Georgia lurched down the stone stairs and fairly flew across the rolling lawn, which Carter was sure wasn't easy considering her shoes sported spike heels and ridiculous pointy toes.

Behind them on the verandah, the first frantic shouts came from the crowd. "Hey! It looks like that tablecloth is on fire. *Fire!* Fire? *Fire!* Someone, quickly! It's spreading! *Throw water on it! Fire!*"

"Carter, *stop!*" Panting, Georgia squatted down, dug in her heels and skidded across the lawn.

Finally Carter realized that she wasn't cooperating and stopped tugging. Without ceremony, he turned around, bent low, placed his shoulder in Georgia's abdomen and stood, rendering her a speechless rag doll. As she flopped along he said, "Lady, you've got no choice. You're coming with me."

After what seemed to Georgia like an eon spent bouncing along on his shoulder as he trekked over Big Daddy's golf course of a lawn, Carter finally dropped her, kicking and screaming on her feet in the middle of a bramble bush, nauseated, dizzy and mad as a hornet. Near as she could tell, they were at the edge of the area Big Daddy affectionately called the Hundred Acre Woods.

"What the *hell* do you think you're doing? Do you have any idea how much this dress cost me?"

"You can't stay here at the Circle BO. And, please, keep your voice down or they may hear you."

"They?" Arms gesticulating wildly, she hissed, "*Who* they? *What* they? Where are *they?*"

"How...Seuss." Carter said drolly as he reached up and fingered the stem of his outsize glasses. "Vander-housen, here."

Georgia snorted. *What the devil was he doing introducing himself to her now?* Hands to hips, she tossed her head and snapped, "I *know* who you are."

"Shhh." Holding his forefinger to his mouth, he closed his eyes and seemed to concentrate. "Yes. We've got a problem."

"I know we have a prob—"

Clearly annoyed, Carter held up the palm of his hand to her face and continued. "Yes, and I think they may have taken a hostage. A guy named Brandon McGraw. Big *M* little *c*. Right."

*"Hostage?"* Georgia stomped her foot. "Are you talking to me or the little people in your head? Carter, I want to know where Brandon is, and I want to know *now!*"

"He led them to believe he was involved. No. I have someone with me. A woman. Georgia Brubaker. Right. Good. Make all the necessary arrangements and I'll fill you in when I get to you." Carter opened his eyes and seemed to stare into the distance. "Go ahead and zap the coordinates. Got 'em. Yeah, I can see it on the e-zone. Fine. I'm gone." After he touched the stem of his glasses one last time, he held out his hand to Georgia. "Come on. We have to leave here immediately."

*"What?* That's ridiculous. I'm not going anywhere. I promised my aunt I'd stay *here* and play hostess to you. So, stop all this Neo Matrix nonsense and let's go back to what is now most likely one hellacious barbecue."

"No."

"No?" *Oh, why had she confided her insane suspicions to a Trekkie like Cootie?*

"No."

Georgia sighed. Okay, assertiveness did not work with him. She'd play on his emotions. If he had any. "Carter, please. Listen. Miss Clarise has planned this evening for ages. If I leave and abdicate my duties as hostess to your family, she'll kill me."

Carter helped her out of the bushes and dusted her off the best he could without getting too personal. "Under the circumstances, your aunt won't mind if you come with me."

"Okay." Georgia issued some incredulous laughter and scratched her head. "I don't know what kind of medication you are on, but trust me when I tell—"

"Georgia, for once, you have to trust *me*. You may have inadvertently stepped into something that could put you in harm's way. It's my job to keep you out of harm's way."

*Whoo boy.*

There he went again, acting all "Bond, James Bond" to impress her. If it wasn't so maddening, she'd laugh. "Cootie Biggles?" she taunted. "Savin' little ol' me? From what? Some drunkin' boogeymen?" Georgia groaned as he took her by the wrist and yanked her through the perimeter of the woods toward the pasture Big Daddy had set up as a parking lot. "Honestly, you don't have to try so hard to impress…okay, where are we going?"

"My car. Where you'll be safe."

"Your *car?* Wait just a doggone minute! Are you serious? You *are* serious! Carter, now you're really starting to scare me. What do you mean you're going to keep me *safe?*"

There was no way she was getting into a car and going anywhere with this lunatic. She watched TV. She knew a homicidal maniac when she saw one. This guy fit the MO to a T. Bullied as a kid. Obsessed with her. Delusional.

"I'm going to try to keep you alive."

"*Me?* What'd I do?" She had to talk him out of taking her off the property. "Carter, listen to me. My sister? You remember her? Ginny? Well, she's a doctor now. Actually, she's a psychologist and a darn good one, too. I'd really like for you to talk to her. In fact, she's back there, at the par—"

"Shh." Carter froze, listening, staring, concentrating. Moments later, after he seemed to receive the all clear from some nebulous—and irritatingly invisible—source, he gripped her, this time by both arms. She pulled back but was amazed to discover that his grasp was as steely as a vise. The only way she was likely to escape was to leave her arms behind.

After a careful surveillance of the area, Carter cautiously emerged from the woods into the countrified parking lot with a stumbling Georgia in tow.

"Don't say a word." The grim caution in his voice brooked no argument.

No problem. She was too petrified to speak. Tiny bleats of fear worked their way up Georgia's throat and past her lips as they cautiously proceeded toward wherever it was Carter had parked his car. The stubble from newly mown hay caught at her skirts, hopelessly snagging the smooth material and at the same time shredding her stockings. Her purse dangled from her shoulder and thumped at her hip. If he would only let go of her hands, she could open it and scatter the contents so that searchers would begin to know where to look for her body.

The sound of a rapid flapping just overhead had Georgia ducking. She whimpered. Was it a bat? Carter didn't seem to notice and forged on. It was probably one of his kinfolk, out looking for a fresh neck.

Georgia's heart vibrated a hundred miles per hour beneath her ribs and her breath came in short, panicky puffs. She was hot and itchy from their recent sprint, and the beginnings of a whopping side ache began to throb just beneath her diaphragm. Off in the distance, rumbling generators powered bright lights to illuminate the many rows of cars, but even so, the shadows were deep and seemed to be crawling with danger.

As Georgia stumbled along behind Carter, a shot suddenly rang out from somewhere behind them, and with a guttural cry of terror Georgia—acting on instinct, as she had since she'd attended grade school with Cootie—flew at his back and dragged them both to the ground.

# Chapter Four

"Would you mind telling me just what it is that you are doing?" Carter asked, his tone as dry as the crunchy pasture beneath his face.

"*Yes*. It would seem that I am *trying*—" gripping the collar on the back of his shirt, Georgia scrambled up beside him, brought her lips to his ear and hissed "—to protect your sorry butt from the *bullies. Again!* In case you hadn't noticed—" covertly she scoured the area for the sniper "—*someone is shooting at you!*"

He craned his head over his shoulder to better peer up at her. "Georgia." Her name came out on a long-suffering puff that had the hair surrounding her face fluttering. "That was a car backfiring."

"How do *you* know?"

"Because—"

A deafening *bang* sounded once again, just over their heads. Carter winced. And not because the noise was so loud, but rather because Georgia had clambered onto his back and had great gobs of his hair clutched in a death grip between her fingers.

Carter cleared his throat and began again. "As I was saying, I know it's a backfire, because it came from that car. The one driving slowly by us now. Right there."

*Bang!*

He strained up onto his elbows and pointed. "See? Wave to the Moorlands."

Mortified, Georgia hid her face in his neck.

"Yes. Oh, look," he grunted. "They're wavin' back. A little puzzled as to why you should be lying on top of me in the middle of the parking lot this way, but they're smiling. Oh, yeah." Carter nodded and smiled back as the elderly couple slowly tooled by.

*Bang.*

*Bang, bang!*

The sound of their engine and the ensuing backfire grew distant as they drove away.

"Ah, but don't you worry your pretty head 'bout them. Probably just figured you couldn't wait to throw me down and start tearing at my clothes and hair…ouch, could ya loosen your grip there?"

"Serves you right." Georgia let go of his hair and cuffed him upside the head. "Yes. Well." She harrumphed and rolled from his back to the ground and landed in an undignified heap. "It sounded like gunfire to me."

"You get shot at pretty frequently?"

"Buzz off."

"Remind me to teach you the difference between minor engine problems and gunfire." Carter rolled over, slowly sat up and tugged the high heel of her shoe out of his sock. Then, pulling himself to his feet, he brushed off his pants and offered her a hand. "In any event, thank you for trying to save my life, but next time—" his voice carried a vaguely patronizing note "—leave the heroics to somebody who knows what they're doing."

"Like you?" she guffawed, and slapped his hand away. "The kid most likely to die from injuries sustained during a rousing game of chess?"

"Y'know—" he ran his hand over his jaw and muttered "—I knew I talked too much. Coulda kept my big fat trap shut. But, no. I just couldn't resist showing off in front of Georgia Brubaker. The one little girl I've wanted to impress since I was three years old."

"Oh, you impress me, all right."

"Let's go."

Georgia struggled to her feet and began picking the wheat stubble from her hair. "No. Wait. Before you take me for another trip down fantasy lane, I demand that you tell me what's up with this idiotic game of hide and seek we seem to be playing with—" brows aloft, palms skyward, she looked around "—no one!"

"As I told you before, we are going to find out what's keeping your boyfriend. Come on." He caught her by the wrist and yanked her along behind him. "We haven't got all day."

"I said wait!" She groped for reasons to stall. "What if you were right? What if he's simply gone to the bathroom?"

"Nope. Not there."

"How do you know?" She jeered at him. "Did you ask your glasses?"

"As a matter of fact, yes." A few quick strides took them to a beautiful, cherry-red sports car, and again Carter touched the frame of his glasses. The doors silently powered open and he pushed Georgia toward the passenger side. "Get in."

"But…but—"

"Get *in*."

Before she could sputter any further, Georgia found herself buckled into a seat beside Carter inside the most amazing vehicle she'd ever seen. As he inserted the key, the horses under the hood seemed to spring to life, and the front end of the car literally lifted off the ground, as if it were ready and rearing to go. Jaw sagging, eyes wide as saucers, Georgia's dull gaze swept what could only be described as a jumbo jet's cockpit. *Wow.* She shifted her focus to Carter who did not seem unduly impressed with his ride. Georgia frowned as realization dawned. Why, he must drive this thing everyday.

Cootie Biggles? In the Batmobile?

The dashboard looked as if it had been invented by "Q" himself and sported gewgaws and gadgets that surely had nothing to do with driving. As she stared at the dizzying array of electronics, Carter peeled off his thick glasses, tossed them in the back seat and selected a button on the dash that turned the rearview mirror into a small, oblong computer monitor. The touch of another button had him placing a phone call.

"*Who* are you calling?" Georgia twisted around in her seat and watched the scenery go by as the car began to roll through the pasture.

"Shhh."

A voice on the speakerphone picked up on the first ring as Carter shifted gears and built speed. When he came to the end of the makeshift road, he tore out of the pasture, down the mile-long Brubaker driveway and onto the highway.

A female voice answered. "Federal Bureau of Intelligence."

"*Wha—?*" Georgia gasped.

Carter and the woman exchanged brief pleasantries before he was transferred several times and finally got down to business. "Stand by to record evidence in case number Alpha, Zebra, Charlie, Zero, Niner, Two."

"I'll transfer you to that mailbox." A series of electronic beeps sounded and then another woman's soft voice answered. "Standing by to record evidence in case number AZC092 after the tone."

Georgia's hands circled her throat. "*The FBI?* What on earth have you people done with Brandon?"

"Don't worry, we'll get your boyfriend back. Now—" He adjusted a lever as a long tone sounded over the speaker. "Once again, repeat to me everything you overheard. And speak clearly into the ashtray."

"Are you *kidding?*"

"Do I *look* like I'm kidding?"

Georgia swallowed. No. He looked serious. Dead serious. Rolling her eyes, she began her bizarre tale, taking care to address the ashtray.

Carter nodded along as she spoke, splitting his attention between her story and the highway. He changed lanes often, accelerating and then downshifting and then accelerating again as he navigated them to points unknown. When she had finished her tale, he slammed the ashtray shut and patted her knee. "Good job."

Yes. She guessed as far as conversations with receptacles for cigarette butts went, this one was right jolly.

Given that this was a weeknight—at the tail end of rush hour to boot—traffic was a zoo. And of course Carter drove like he did everything else: with an intensity that had her cringing in fear. Georgia grabbed for the passenger handles, one over her window on the right, and one on the left, near the brake. Reciting the serenity prayer, she held on for dear life.

An alarm suddenly began to flash on the dash, and the muscles in Carter's face tensed with his apparent irritation. "I was afraid this would happen." He activated a small video monitor on his visor and, with a remote control, zoomed in on a speeding black sedan.

"What? What is happening? You are really scaring the pea-waddin' outta me."

So intensely was he concentrating, Carter's face scarcely registered that he'd heard.

"Cootie Biggles, if you don't tell me what you are up to, I swear I'll jump out of this car and hitch a ride home."

"We are going over a hundred miles an hour."

"You *know*..." Georgia pressed her lips together and fumed as she peered out the window. "Where the *devil* are the cops when you *really* need them?" She turned and glared at him. "I don't care how fast we're going. I guess I'll just have to hitch a ride back with an ambulance."

At this dire proclamation, Carter seemed to come to a conclusion. "Okay. But you have to promise that what I tell you now will never go any further than right here."

Her arm smacked into the window as she waved wild hands. "Who the *heck* am I going to *tell?*"

They raced along through the darkness in silence for a moment.

"Promise?"

"Yes. Stick a finger in my eye and all that rot."

"Pinkie-swear?" Carter grinned, mocking her deal with Brandon.

"Just talk. I'll never, ever tell anyone. I promise." Not that anyone would ever believe her if she did recount this idiotic escapade.

"All right. First of all, you should know that I work for—" The alarm sounded again, this time more insistently. *"Dammit."* Carter glanced at the video monitor and then at the computer in the rearview mirror.

Georgia froze. "What does that mean?" When he didn't immediately answer, she huffed and held out her little finger. "Okay. I pinkie-swear."

Her stomach lurched into her throat as Carter suddenly cranked the steering wheel, stomped on the breaks and spun the car 180 degrees in the middle of a four-lane freeway. When Georgia had stopped screaming and opened her eyes, they were abruptly flying in the opposite direction.

"What, in the name of all that is sanity, are you *doing?*"

"We have a tail."

"A what?"

"Someone is following us." Carter got on his secure phone. "We're being followed." He listened. "Yeah." He checked the instruments on his dash, noting coordinates and degrees horizontal and vertical on his screen with a stylus. "Can do. We are headed north to north east. Jubilee Truck Stop. Check. Right. Give me three…no two and five-eighths minutes."

As Carter once again reached speeds over a hundred miles an hour, Georgia reached similar levels on the decibel chart with her squeals. He didn't seem to even be *looking* as he tore up the road, zipping in and out of the heavy traffic, at times traveling on the shoulder or median. She slapped her hands over her eyes, but unable to resist the morbid fascination, peered through the slits between her fingers.

"Cootie! *Stop!* Please!" Georgia felt as if she was begging for her life. "Let me out. I understand you had a hard time as a child. People bullied you. You want to be admired. But really, isn't this just a tad—" she burbled some hysterical laughter "—over the top? I mean, *years* have passed.

Most of those people don't even remember you, I'm sure. Seriously, you need help. My sister, the one I was telling you about, is a wonderful psycholo—"

"Georgia, this has nothing to do with my childhood, so you can stop probing my psyche." Again, Carter hit the brakes, performing another 180 just as a semi-trailer passed them going the opposite direction.

"*Ohhhhhh.*" Georgia ducked and, assuming crash position, covered her head. In little pants she whimpered to herself. *"Heeeee'sssss craaaazy!* Out of his ever-lovin' *gourd.* Certifiable. Has me talking to ashtrays. People are out to get him. *Ohh…*he's paranoid. Delusional. I can't remember what Ginny says to do to calm people like you." She peeked over at him and asked meekly, "Cootie, could I please borrow your ashtray? I need to call my sister."

A sudden and hellacious scraping noise had Georgia jerking her focus up and out the windshield. She fell back against her seat and cringed in terror at what she saw looming ahead.

Rising before them, the semi they'd just passed—and then spun to follow—had lowered its trailer gate. It was now bouncing and scraping along on the ground before them, shooting fireworks at their windshield à la Fourth of July. Before Georgia could even blink, Carter gunned the engine and drove up onto the sparking ramp and into the trailer.

Two men, dressed entirely in black, hauled the door closed. And, as if he were here for a day at the mall, Carter expertly parked the car next to several others toward the front of the trailer and cut the engine. Quietly, his tinted window hummed down. One of the men in black approached.

"You lost 'em."

"*You?*" Georgia stared at Carter. "You're the…*phantom?*" Slumping against her door, she slipped from consciousness.

* * *

"Who's the woman?"

"A very old and very dear friend." Carter looked on as Georgia lay sprawled in the seat next to him, for once not yapping a mile a minute. She was so beautiful. A tender fondness welled up in his throat, and he reached out to adjust her seat to a more comfortable reclining position.

"She doesn't look old. She looks hot."

Carter squinted over his shoulder at his longtime co-worker and buddy, warning him off. "Yeah, well don't get any ideas, Marsh. She's taken. That goes for you, too, Zach," he called after the second black-clad man.

"Yeah, yeah." Marshall lifted his palm. "We get it. You get all the good ones. So, what's the deal?"

"They've got moles out snooping. Came a little too close for comfort tonight."

"We knew it was only a matter of time."

"Yeah." Carter slipped off his seat belt and got out of the car. "Come on. I'll brief you while I shave."

"What about her?"

"Let her rest. She's gonna need it. Zach! Get her a bottle of water and let me know when she comes to, okay?"

"My extreme pleasure."

Carter shot him a narrow look as he pulled back the curtain that shielded the tiny bathroom facilities. He scanned the cubbies for his shaving kit. There it was. Just where he'd left it two months ago. He grabbed a can of shaving cream and a razor and went to work on his beard as he filled Marshall in on all the details that this evening had wrought.

"So, let me understand. You believe they might have her boyfriend and so far you don't think they connected the dots to you?" Marshall asked.

"Clearly, they wonder why I left with Brandon's woman, and are no doubt suspicious about me."

"Fine. We're ready. In the meantime, you need to disappear."

Carter picked up a pair of scissors and began cutting his hair short. "Yeah."

"You taking her with you?"

"I don't have much choice, do I?"

"Not at this point. Unless you want to leave her with Zach and me." Marshall lifted a roguish brow.

"Funny."

"In that case, we'll get you loaded for two. Will a week's supplies be sufficient?"

"I'd think so."

"Good. There are maps to secure areas being downloaded onto your e-zone now. I'll go check on 'em."

"Great."

After a few moments of silent organization by the small crew, Marshall returned. "She's still out. Pulse rate normal, breathing fine. Looks like an angel when she sleeps."

"Yeah. I remember from naptime in kindergarten."

"You two *do* go back."

Carter only grunted and handed him a pair of clippers. "Take a little off the sides and back while you fill me in on what the guys at headquarters know, huh?"

"Sure." With an expertise born of long experience, Marshall skillfully changed Carter's appearance, first with the clippers, then with peroxide.

"Blond?" Carter groaned and ran his hand over the golden tips now spiking the top of his head. "You've got to be kidding."

"They saw you as a scruffy absentminded wildebeest before. They won't be looking for a surfer dude. Here are your new glasses." Marshall handed Carter a stylish pair of sunglasses. "They work exactly like the others and, though they look like dark glasses, they function just as precisely in low light. Perfect for your new persona. They are your constant connection to us, so don't lose them."

"Check." Carter stood and dusted the hair off his shoulders and chest, then stretched a fresh T-shirt on over his head and tucked it into his jeans. He looked down at the logo emblazoned across his chest. "'Let's Body Surf?' What kind of superdork am I supposed to be now?"

Marsh grinned. "Sorry. Since we didn't expect you tonight, it was that or I'm With Stupid. The rest of your wardrobe is a little more dialed down."

Carter snorted. "I gotta get moving. Anything else?"

"Yes. You have reservations under the name Sanders when you arrive at the motel. First name, Keith, for you and Lori for your…friend. We told them you're on your honeymoon and will require complete privacy."

"Gotcha. Where?"

"It's on the e-zone. A little backwater town *waaaaay* out in the sticks. Your new IDs and credit cards are in your wallet. You'll find luggage with fresh sets of clothes for you both packed in the trunk. You have enough camping gear and MREs to get you through for over a week, though we hope it won't be that long." Marshall clapped him on the back. "We will notify you as soon as we know anything about Brandon and the syndicate that may have abducted him. Until then, take care and good luck."

Finally Georgia began her slow ascent toward quasi consciousness from her horrible, episodic nightmare. *Oh.* She moaned a little and ran her tongue over her dry lips and swallowed. It had been so awful. Thank God it was just a dream. It was dark. She could feel the night through her eyelids. She stretched, feeling reasonably comfortable. And warm. And…covered by a light blanket? Odd. Especially since she was beginning to realize that she was not in her own bed. Where was she? She frowned as she struggled to organize her thoughts.

From the sound and feel of things, she was sitting in a car.

A car?

Why would she be in a car? The engine was running, but the car didn't seem to be moving.

With great reluctance she pried open her eyes and peered through her lashes. Yes. She was in the front passenger seat of a car. Her head rolled left. A car whose driver was a very handsome man she'd never met. When this fully registered, a jolt of terror thundered through Georgia and erupted from her mouth in the form of a blood-curdling scream.

"Who are you?" she gasped, jerking upright so that she could better hyperventilate.

"I thought you said introductions were not necessary." The droll voice was familiar and had Georgia blinking at its owner.

"Cootie?"

He shrugged as he went over what looked like a clipboard holding a pilot's flight plan and adjusted dials and knobs accordingly. "Phantom, Cootie, whatever."

"What happened to you? You look…you look—" she peered through the shadows at his face, illuminated by the soft light of his dashboard "—you look so different."

"Got a haircut and a shave."

Georgia could only gape in amazement. It sounded like Cootie. But he looked so…so…normal.

"How are you feeling?"

She bristled and groped for the lever that would put her seat back upright. "How do you *think* I'm feeling?"

He grinned. "Never mind. I'll take care of that for you." At the push of a button, her seat quietly moved up and she sat stiffly, her back barely touching the lush padding.

"This is not the same car."

"No."

She glanced around. They were still in the trailer. That would account for the engine noise and the sensations of motion. Her gaze skimmed the dash. This car seemed just as high-tech as the other, but the interior was black leather, matching the exterior paint job. The car they'd driven in was still in the trailer, parked in front of them now. Seemed there was money in the phantom business. "Just how long was I out?"

"About half an hour." When he'd finished with his pre-flight check, he nodded at the two men who'd let them in, started the engine and then began backing toward the gate they were lowering. Again, as the gate contacted the pavement, sparks flew and the noise was horrendous.

A silent scream built and froze in Georgia's open mouth. If she lived through this night, she was gonna kill Cootie Biggles.

There was a terrible jolt as the back tires hit the pavement. The opposing forces caught the wheels and the car fishtailed as if they'd hit a patch of ice. Unfazed, Carter steered out of the crisis and, easing onto the shoulder, built speed until he was able to cross the ditch at a narrow point and cut across a field. Eventually, the field led to a dirt road that led to a paved road that led to a highway that led to—Georgia pulled her lower lip between her teeth—only heaven knew where.

Miles flowed into endless miles at ungodly speeds and finally Georgia's scream collapsed in her throat, leaving her with a guttural, gurgling exhalation. She covered her face with her hands. Was this how he drove everywhere? The stress was going to kill her. "Please, oh, please just tell me where we are going," she ventured when she had finally calmed down enough to hear over the pounding of her heart.

"Somewhere safe."

"Oh, that is just so…comforting." Sudden exasperation had Georgia jamming her arms together across her chest. "You know, I think you owe me more than a bogus two-word explanation."

"You're right."

"I demand that you tell me not only where we are going, but who we are running from."

"Okay."

"And who on earth were those yahoos back there in that truck? And how did they know you'd be coming by? And another thing—"

"Georgia."

"—why did we switch cars? And why did you cut your hair? And what—"

"Georgia!"

"—about Brandon? What about *him?* Do you think for one minute that I'm just going to—"

"Georgia!"

"What?"

"Shut up."

Her mouth sagged.

"I'll tell you everything you want to know, if you'd only let me get a word in edgewise."

"Fine." Chagrined, she waved a hand in his direction. "Go ahead, then."

"Okay." He emitted a long, deep sigh, and Georgia knew he was trying to find a spot in this mess, to begin.

While she waited, she took advantage of the excuse to look him up one side and down the other. She simply couldn't get over the sudden and complete difference in his appearance. Incredible what a new hairstyle and a shave could do for a guy. That, and some casual clothes that actually fitted, and well, she pinched her lips between her thumb and forefinger, he was actually quite handsome. Quite.

He looked just like, in fact he looked *exactly* like that one guy, oh, heck, he could be twin brothers with him, that guy…oh, that guy from that TV show. Oh, it was someone…someone she'd just seen the other day…oh *shoot,* she hated that. Now that was gonna bug her until she thought of it.

Carter seemed not to notice that she was somewhat distracted as he launched into his explanation.

"Before I explain the myriad functions of the company I own, it might be helpful for you to understand the problem we are dealing with, and then I'll go into how my business fits into the scheme of things."

"Mmm." Eyes glazed, Georgia nodded. He didn't play a doctor or a cop. It wasn't a sitcom. But it wasn't a drama, either.

"All right. As you are probably well aware, petroleum and its many by-products have a wide and varied effect on practically every aspect of our culture. I'm assuming that all your life, you've been told that oil is the most viable option for transportation fuel."

"Mmm-hmm."

"Me, too. But that's not necessarily true anymore. Researchers are finding other, earth-friendly, not to mention renewable options that could be cleaner, more fuel efficient and maybe even less expensive than oil."

"Mmm." Oh, this was going to drive her crazy. Who, who, *who* did he look like?

As Carter settled back in his seat and steered down the straight road with a wrist dangling over the wheel, Georgia strained toward him, scrutinizing every aspect of his mature profile as he expounded on a subject that was clearly dear to his heart. She could see the reflections of his once youthful parents. He had Harlan's strong jaw and lanky, sinewy stature, and Daisy's full, deeply bracketed lips and exotic eyes. The pleasing attributes he'd inherited from each of his parents had melded together and taken him from a goofy-looking kid to a remarkably handsome man. That is, when he wasn't hiding behind ten pounds of hair and glasses.

"—can tell that you already understand that dynamic." He shot her an admiring grin that spoke of his appreciation for her diligent attention. "So, of course, that doesn't bode well for future generations. Unfortunately, there is big money involved in the weaning process and special-interest groups are intent on keeping things the way they are. However, even those people are beginning to realize that the U.S. cannot stay dependant on the Middle East for oil forever. And the sooner we can orient our dependency away from the OPEC nations, the sooner we can begin the conversion process."

"Mmm-hmm." What conversion process? What was he talking about? Her gaze landed on his lips as he spoke. Such mobile, pliable lips. Why on earth had he hidden them under that scruffy Grizzly-Adams-without-a-clue look? His upper lip curled in the middle, giving his grin a most irreverent quality. In his right cheek, there was a tiny dimple that appeared with certain words, but she'd need to study that a lot longer to figure out exactly which words those were....

He had really great teeth. Last time she'd seen him, many of his permanent teeth were still on their way in. Absently she wondered if he'd had to wear braces when he was a kid. People with teeth that straight usually had.

Her gaze dipped to watch his bicep flex as he steered around a corner in the road, and it struck her that the dumb black T-shirt he was wearing looked pretty good on him. He wasn't ready for the cover of *Muscle Magazine* by any stretch, but he had a surprisingly decent build. Exactly the kind she liked. Lean. Sinewy. Masculine. Very nice.

Very weird.

"And, yes, it will be expensive, it will be done incrementally, and it will take years. And, of course, there are people out there who don't want it done at all. Not just the men at Big Daddy's party, but people who hold oil interests everywhere. And some of these folks—as in any group where big money is involved—are dangerous people."

*"Yes!"* Georgia slapped her forehead with the palm of her hand. *That was it!* He looked just like that really cute, really goofy carpenter from one of those reality home-decorating shows. She loved that show. She—and practically every breathing female in America—loved that carpenter. He could build anything. Fix anything. And he was funny to boot. Just like Carter. The resemblance was uncanny.

Oh, man, what a relief! She sagged against the back of her seat and blew out a noisy exhale. Now she could relax and concentrate on whatever it was Carter was blathering on about.

"Yeah," Carter nodded, misreading her verbal explosion as some kind of lightbulb popping on over her head regarding the worldwide future of fuel. "You're right. And that's precisely why we're on the lam right now."

"It is?"

"Yep."

"We are? On the *lam?*"

"Uh-huh."

Criminettely. Georgia twisted some flyaway strands of hair around her fingertip. On the lam from what? Words like *world economy* and *OPEC* and *global warming* swirled through her head but made no real sense. Why hadn't she paid better attention to everything he just said? She could hardly ask him to repeat it, especially since he was glowing over her apparent ability to fathom complex political ideology.

"I know," Carter commiserated. "It's a lot to take in, huh?"

"Yeah." Georgia nodded and glanced out her window. It sure was.

"Anyway, we're here."

"Here?" Georgia blinked. They were? Where was here?

Carter pointed up at the rather dilapidated marquee that read:

MOTEL TOAD
Toad Suck, Texas.
Deluxe rooms, low rates
$H_2O$ beds, A/C, Cable TV
Vacancy

"Come on," he said, and—while she was still digesting the fact that she was in a town that someone had actually thought to name Toad Suck for crying in the night—grabbed some luggage from his trunk and nodded for her to follow him into the shabby lobby.

"Hey." He handed his credit card to the tiny, blue-haired woman who sat behind the counter, smoking like a chimney and cackling at the miniature TV blaring from behind the counter.

"Shh." Without looking up, she waved at Carter and began to process his card. "Stupid pet tricks. Hang on." As a cockatoo refused to whistle *Dixie* while its owner plied it with treats, the hotel clerk sucked her cigarette till the ash was a good inch long. Finally, as the late-night program went into a commercial break, the clerk swore at the TV then turned her attention to her customer. "I hate the birds. They never do what you tell 'em to. I ask ya, what's cuddly about a damned bird?"

Carter shrugged. "Dunno. I got a reservation."

"So." She tossed his credit card back. "You're Keith Sanders."

"Yeah. And this is Lori."

"Been expectin' ya. You're the first reservation we've had in ages. Honeymoon, huh?"

"Yeah."

Georgia's eyes widened. Honeymoon? Was *that* what was he was telling this clerk? That they were *newlyweds?*

"You're honeymooning in Toad Suck? You crazy? You should go to Vegas." The wizened woman tossed a key at Carter with one hand and stubbed out her cigarette with the other.

"We want privacy." Carter tucked the key into his back pocket.

"You got it, honey. You guys are it this week. Room eight, down that way." She pointed with the glowing end of her cigarette. "It's our only honeymoon suite. Got a great view of the train tracks. Real romantic." She focused her watery gaze on Georgia. "Honey, you must really love this idiot to put up with a honeymoon in this dive."

"Oh, she does." Carter reached for Georgia's arm as

she began to back away and yanked her up close. "Don'cha, hon?"

"I...but...we can't stay in the same—"

Carter brought his nose to Georgia's. "Sure we can, sweetheart."

"What's wrong?" The clerk lit another cigarette.

"Nothing." Carter lightly touched his lips to Georgia's and she stared up at him in shock. "Now don't you go fretting about not packing enough clothes." To the old woman he said, "She hates to *stay* in the *same* clothes. But I keep telling her we're not gonna need our clothes."

The night clerk cackled, seeming to find them more interesting than the skateboarding dog. Ashes and butts flew as her reedy hoots of laughter scattered the contents of the ashtray. "That's for damn sure."

"But...but..." Georgia protested and planted her hands on his chest. She couldn't think with his lips so close. But if there was one thing she knew, it was that she couldn't stay in the same room with Carter. It not only wasn't decent, it—

Carter grabbed her wrists and pinned them between their bodies. "Sweetheart, really, you just have to stop all this silly worry and trust me." His suddenly dark eyes carried a don't-mess-with-me warning that had goose bumps crawling up her spine.

Her lips fell slack and her breathing became shallow. "But—"

Carter cut her off with another quick kiss. "No buts," he insisted, and then kissed her again. This time with feeling.

# Chapter Five

Without regard for their chain-smoking audience, Carter hauled Georgia flush against him and gave her the kiss she'd thought she wanted from Brandon earlier that afternoon. But she'd been mistaken if she thought Brandon was capable of ever making her feel like *this*.

This was...oh, this was... Words escaped her.

Carter had inserted his leg between hers and with a hand at her lower back, tilted her slightly so that she was completely dependant on him for balance. With his other hand, he gripped her wrists at his chest, while he explored her mouth with his, nipping and tasting and urging her to respond.

Though the original intent was clearly to keep her from talking, Georgia's mind went blank, and instinct took over. The lush, full-bodied kiss slowly changed in tenor from protest to curiosity. And from there it morphed into something that began to satisfy an age-old ache that had plagued her forever.

Until now.

Now, for the first time in her life, Georgia was *in* the moment. Not beside it, not near it, but *in* it. Fully. Completely. With pounding heart and laboring lungs. What had begun as a tiny tingling sensation in the pit of her belly, smoldered and flared to life as he tilted her chin and slowly moved his lips over hers. Everything she'd imagined a kiss could be was suddenly real. The sensations were marvelous and sumptuous and didn't stop at the mere point where their lips met.

Chills, like the tiny feet of so many fairies, danced up and down her spine, and the strangest symptoms assailed her body, all foreign, all beyond pleasant. Was this what all the poetry was about? The fairy tales? The thing some people had actually killed for to possess? Suddenly it all became so clear.

Yes.

Years of waiting for this exact ecstasy had only built tinder for the fire. With a mind blank to everything but the feel of Carter's body pressed tightly against hers, Georgia gave herself up to the excitement he kindled.

How could this be?

It was like smacking headfirst into the end of the rainbow and tripping over the pot of gold. All this time it was right here under her nose. Paradise.

In Carter's kiss.

Magnificent. Delightful.

Absurd.

He let go of her wrists and of their own volition her arms slipped behind his back, where her palms explored the sinewy planes beneath his T-shirt. He was soft and steely and she snuggled closer to run her hands along the breadth of his shoulders. Fingers sliding lower, up and over his arms, she curled them around his biceps and allowed her head to drop back to give Carter access to her mouth, her jaw, her neck, her throat and then her mouth again.

The night clerk forgot she was already smoking and lit another cigarette.

Georgia was oblivious to the blue haze that coiled from the ashtray. Oblivious to the warped trailer paneling, the threadbare carpeting, the water stains that marred the ceiling, the dusty plastic foliage. She was oblivious to the laugh track that blared from the tiny TV and oblivious to the staring night clerk and oblivious to, well, to…everything.

Everything but the electricity in her body. The jungle beat in her ears. The feeling that she was being consumed by, and addicted to, something over which she had no power. Little mewling whimpers sounded in her throat, and her knees were so weak she feared that if Carter released his hold, she'd slip to the floor and lie there in a daze.

Slowly, ever so slowly, Carter pulled his mouth away from Georgia's. His breath was as labored as hers, and she could feel a tremor rack his body as he fought for composure.

"You okay?" His lips lightly feathered hers as he spoke.

Georgia swallowed and nodded. Better than okay. She was perfect. Pulsing. Alive. Able to leap tall buildings in a single bound.

"Good." Forehead to forehead, he stood with her for a moment, his eyes closed. "Wow," he murmured.

"Mmm. Wow." Her nose brushed his as she nodded.

With a flick of his tongue, he touched the tiny smile at his lips and sighed. "C'mon. We gotta get out of view."

Not sure if this was because they were being pursued or because he wanted privacy, Georgia didn't know or care.

"Mmm." Arms dangling, head spinning, she simply stood there, dazed.

Cootie Biggles had just kissed her.

And she would never be the same again.

Ecstasy soon became agony as Carter inserted the key into the rusty bolt lock and let them into the Motel Toad's so-called honeymoon suite. Once they were inside the door, he flipped on the wall switch. The sudden blast of light had the cockroaches scurrying for cover.

Georgia screamed and clutched Carter's arm.

"Shh." He closed the door, threw the bolt, then moved to the window and drew the blinds. "It's okay. They won't hurt you."

"I can't sleep in a room full of bugs," Georgia whimpered and shadowed his every move as he checked the room over for anything unusual.

"I don't know. It beats sleeping outside."

"It does not! Here, we're locked *in* with the bugs."

"Good point."

Her skin crawled as she balefully surveyed the honeymoon cave where she was to spend the night. Did real people actually stay here? On their wedding nights, no less? How dismal. It was every bit as ugly as the lobby, and Georgia was pretty sure the stench of mold and stale smoke would only disappear with the razing of the building.

"I know," she whispered as she tiptoed after Carter, "that you are used to sleeping in the jungle and being detained in foreign prisons and stuff like that, but I'm—"

She paused as the greasy shag carpet beneath her feet began to vibrate. Soon the bug cemetery in the chandelier was bouncing. Then swaying. The walls shimmied and the water glasses and ice bucket rattled about on top of the TV.

A rumble began off in the distance and grew till it reached the proportions of a thunderstorm that blotted out her own primal scream.

*"Tornado! Earthquake! Tsunami!"* She jumped at Carter and buried her face in his chest as blinding flashes of lightning suddenly filled the room. She twisted his shirt in her fists and, sobbing into the folds, waited for the blast that would sweep her into oblivion. Clearly, the four horsemen of the apocalypse were galloping across the sky overhead.

It was the end of the world.

And here she was in Toad Suck, about to die in a seedy, cockroach-infested motel room with Cootie Biggles. She sniffed as her life flashed before her eyes for the second or third time that day. Somehow, with Carter's arms holding her tight, facing death didn't seem all that horrible. She guessed if she had to endure the end of the world with someone, it might as well be someone whose kiss made her forget all reason. She dabbed her eyes on his shirt and, slowly growing philosophical, supposed there were worse ways to go.

Dying of boredom was one.

She'd been doing that all summer, praying for something exciting to happen to her. And when it did, all she could do was cower. What a weenie. When had she become so consumed by her fears? When had he become so brave? As he cradled her head in the palm of his hand, she could feel the vibration of his voice resonate in his chest as he murmured words meant to soothe.

When had their roles reversed?

The man had ice in his veins. Didn't anything ever upset him? Cause him to lose his cool? The horrible treatment he'd endured as a kid must have made him tough as nails, because the fact that their room seemed to be exploding at the seams didn't affect his pulse rate. Or his breathing. Or his steady grip on her.

The long, deafening scream of a train whistle suddenly solved the mystery. As they stood huddled together, the locomotive shot by, mere inches from the bathroom wall, causing the windows to woof with the changing air pressure and the room to jolt, as if the train track went through the center of the room.

Finally, after what seemed like the world's record for sheer number of cars an engine could pull and still shatter the sound barrier, the train and the accompanying noise faded off in the distance. Georgia was reluctant to release her grip on Carter. She was an emotional wreck.

"You gonna be okay?" he asked for the second time since they'd arrived in Toad Suck.

"Nooo," she whimpered and gave her head a vehement shake.

Carter stroked her hair. "You'll feel better after we've had a nice long shower and something to eat.

"Mmm-hmm."

Slowly he set her away from his grasp and his eyes met hers in a deep, soul-searching look. "You're very brave. Much more so than I'd ever have guessed."

"No. I'm a wimp."

"Georgia, you are many things, but a wimp has never been one. I learned that about you when we were very small. And I've never forgotten the lessons you taught me about bravery." He tilted her chin, and eyes flashing, his gaze dipped to her lips.

Georgia's heart skipped a beat. Was he going to kiss her again? She hoped so.

He seemed to wrestle with that question for a moment himself before he took a step back. "I'll go get that shower.

If you don't mind, I'll just go first. The…the, uh, the little hairs on my neck are driving me crazy. You wait here."

As she stared at the bathroom door, Georgia could hear the old pipes in the wall begin to honk and rumble as Carter started the water in the shower. From the prehistoric sound of things, people weren't inclined to wash up when they stayed in the old Toad Suck honeymoon suite. Probably too busy fending off the roaches.

She listened to the sounds of Carter preparing for his shower and was aware that he was most likely naked. A naked phantom.

She giggled. Nerves.

Of course he was naked. It was the best way to take a shower. Unless, of course, one was staying at the roach motel. She had to stop thinking about bugs. She shivered and ran her hands over her arms. The night had brought on a bit of a chill, and Georgia's party gown was hardly warm.

She gave the bedding a wary glance, and then stepped over to feel the worn comforter. A light touch told her that the bedding was clammy and the blankets limp. She didn't even want to think what a forensic team might find crawling around under one of those blue lights they used to solve crimes. She took a step back. The original waterbed had been replaced with a lumpy mattress that now boasted coin-operated "magic fingers."

Georgia frowned. Why bother paying? The train provided more than enough vibration for free. Minutes ticked by. Georgia paced. Steam poured out from under the bathroom door. It looked humid in there. She could use a hot shower to relax her. She sighed. There was no way she would sleep a wink tonight. No way.

Occasionally she peeked out the window through the

blinds as she paced by. Nothing. That was good. She guessed.

The bathroom door banged open and Carter poked his head out. "I hate to bother you, but I seem to have forgotten my duffel bag. Could you hand it to me? Right over there." Tightening the towel at his hips, Carter pointed to the stack of luggage he'd deposited on the suitcase stand.

A surreal moment passed as Georgia glanced at his glistening chest. She swallowed and forced her feet to carry her to his bags.

"The blue one."

"This one?"

"Yeah. And while you're at it, you might check out what the guys packed for you in the black one. I'll be out of here in a minute and you can hop in."

"Oh. Okay."

"Don't worry, the rust all poured out after the first minute or so." He grinned.

She smiled back and an awkward moment passed as they stood gazing at each other. A small puddle began to form at Carter's feet. Georgia took a step forward and handed him his bag.

"Thanks."

"You're welcome."

He leaned against the door frame, his duffel dangling from his fingertips. "Sorry about the marriage lie." He dragged his free hand through his hair, ruffling the ends, seeming to attempt to come to terms with his new, shorter 'do.

Georgia watched the play of muscles across his chest and arms as he moved, mesmerized.

"It's just that if they already have Brandon, and you're his business partner and girlfriend—" he swallowed

"—anyway, if they are coming after you, maybe they won't think of looking for a couple."

"Oh, right."

"Don't worry, I'll take the floor."

Georgia glanced at the infestation of orange-and-insect shag carpet and grimaced. He was so brave. Then again, she wasn't overly eager to take the bed. Noting her sour expression, Carter laughed.

"I brought clean bedding. Sterile." He cast a sheepish glance down at his body and ran a hand over his chest, suddenly aware that he was standing there half-dressed. "I'll just go brush my teeth. Then the bathroom is all yours."

The door closed again, and Georgia exhaled a breath she'd been holding. Still convinced that she was in the middle of one whopper of a dream, she opened the black duffel bag and explored its contents.

As Carter swept the room for bugging devices with the equipment that Marshall had provided, he listened to the feminine noises of Georgia taking her shower. After her initial discomfort wore off, she seemed to have forgotten about her surroundings and had even begun to hum under the hot spray. At least the hot water heater still worked.

A small smile played at his lips and he shook his head. She was a trooper. He'd give her that. In his years in the business, Carter hadn't met many women who would have put up with the mayhem this evening had offered and still be humming a cheery ditty at the end of the day.

But then, Georgia Brubaker was an exceptional woman.

While she did whatever it was that women did to prepare for bed, Carter yanked the foul mattress off the bed frame and inflated the camping mattresses that Marshall and Zach had provided. When they were firm, he unfurled the sleeping bags and plumped the pillows. With nothing left to do but wait for Georgia to emerge from the shower, Carter— feeling antsy—grabbed his phone and dialed Marshall.

He had to talk to someone. Had to keep his mind from running over that kiss in his mind. The woman was taken. Not only did she have a boyfriend, but Carter was personally responsible for his safety. He exhaled heavily. A surge of guilt assailed him as he waited for Marshall to pick up. He'd had no business kissing her that way, even if it had worked to convince the clerk that they needed to be left alone.

"Yeah." From the groggy sound of his voice, Carter guessed that Marshall had been asleep.

"Just thought I'd touch base."

"Mmm."

"Thanks for the high-class digs."

Marshall chuckled. "I thought you'd like those. They'll never think to look for her there."

"Got that straight. What's new?"

"Well, just as we suspected, these are guys we've been watching for a long time in connection with a number of criminal activities involving the oil business."

"I had a gut feeling that some of them would be at the Brubaker party tonight. This week, practically everyone in the industry will take part in Big Daddy's 'family reunion.' I knew that. Unfortunately, I allowed myself to be distracted by Georgia."

"Yeah, well, I can see why, after getting a good look at her." Marshall's noisy yawn filled Carter's ear. "Anyway, all things considered, this probably worked out for the best. If they have him, and it looks like it, they've no doubt already figured out that McGraw isn't the guy they're after. They won't hurt him if they decide they can use him to get to you. Luckily, you got a decent head start, and so far you're safe. And so is Georgia. If they kidnapped Brandon McGraw, they made a big mistake tonight. Hopefully, that will finally lead to their arrest and capture."

Carter rubbed his temples and exhaled. "I see your point, but I feel bad about involving McGraw."

"Not your fault."

"Well, actually, it is. I did a little bragging to Georgia."

Silence.

"I knew she still looked at me like the dork I was in pre-school, and it rankled."

Silence.

"Anyway, she must have said something to her boyfriend about our conversation on alternative fuels and this phantom character they were complaining about, because he really seemed to get a charge out of putting those guys on. Goading them. Alluding to the fact that he might be this mysterious phantom."

More silence.

"Marshall?"

"That was dumb."

"Yeah."

"Okay." Marshall groaned. "Well, this puts a whole new spin on things."

"I'm sorry."

"Hey. We knew they were on the lookout for their so-called phantom. It was just a matter of time. Might as well get it over and done with now, rather than wait for them to attack from behind with a car bomb or something."

"They're that bad?"

"Oh, yeah."

"Really. They come across as small-timers."

"They are, but Rocky Klondike's got connections to a huge crime syndicate that we believe is involved in the oil market. He's in the hip pocket of several congressmen across both party lines. So far we haven't been able to pin anything on him, though we've tried. There is at least one unsolved murder in his file."

"What about the others?"

"Nothing yet. Petty stuff in their background checks, but that doesn't necessarily mean anything. All of 'em were last seen about the time Brandon disappeared. If they have Brandon, they've done a pretty good job of hiding him. Unfortunately, until he's been reported missing for more than twenty-four hours, our hands are pretty much tied. But we're looking."

"Yeah." From the bathroom, Carter could hear the water turn off. "Let's just hope they don't skip town with him."

"I don't think they will. Not without Georgia. She's the only one they think could link them to his disappearance. And maybe even to you, depending on what Brandon's told them. No doubt they've launched a full-scale search for her now. You need to lay low."

The hair dryer droned from behind the bathroom door.

Carter ran a hand behind his neck and pinched the tight muscles. Because of him, Georgia was in serious danger. Not to mention Brandon. "Seems I've stirred up a hornet's nest."

"Ah, you're human. Don't beat yourself up too bad. I'll do that when I see you next."

Carter snorted.

"I guess I'm really just surprised it's taken this long for something to happen. I just figured you'd be the one they nabbed."

"Thanks for the vote of confidence."

"Yeah, well anytime." Marshall stifled another yawn.

"Keep me posted."

"Always."

Carter tossed his phone into his duffel bag and stood staring at the bathroom door. As an adult, Georgia was more beautiful than he ever dreamed possible. On the inside as well as the out. No wonder McGraw loved her. The idiot had great taste. Too bad he was all wrong for her.

He sighed, long and heavy.

Story of his life. Always one day late and a dollar short.

Georgia brushed her teeth and hair with the provisions she found in the surprisingly complete toiletry kit the men Carter worked with had put together for her. Absent were luxuries such as makeup, but she'd found a small bottle of hand lotion, a tube of cherry ChapStick and some mint mouthwash. For pajamas they'd provided a pair of running shorts and a T-shirt, both on the large side, but comfy. A pair of sweat socks completed the ensemble and she figured she was ready to face Carter.

Sort of.

A quick glance in the mirror confirmed her fear that her cheeks were fairly blazing with embarrassment.

What on earth did he think of her after the wanton way she'd responded to his kiss? After all, wasn't she supposed to be dating Brandon? She'd certainly made enough noise to that effect over dinner. Making sure that everyone knew they never left each other's side. Not for a second. Certainly not long enough to fall victim to a kidnapper.

Though it wasn't true, talk about appearing fickle.

He must think her a total creep. Georgia buried her face in her palms and moaned. She'd practically devoured Carter right there in the lobby. And what about the way she'd salivated over his dripping body after he'd finished his shower? Lowlife. Loser.

Georgia had always prided herself on exhibiting all of

the Girl Scout virtues. Especially when it came to being trustworthy. And here she'd betrayed Brandon, who could be...*dead.*

Oh, she was such a worm.

Suddenly the reality of their predicament sank in. She snatched the washcloth off the showerhead and plunged it under the icy blast of the faucet. Wringing it out, she mopped the back of her neck, her forehead and her flaming cheeks and battled back an attack of panic.

She had to get a grip.

From now on, she would focus on Brandon and nothing else. Brandon was in danger. She wouldn't allow herself to be distracted by a silly kiss. Or by a smooth, muscular chest. How base. She tossed the washcloth into the sink.

Deep breath. Count to ten.

Okay.

Her exhalation fogged the mirror. So she'd been under a bit of stress and had reacted badly. It wouldn't happen again. Rotating her shoulders and giving her hands a vigorous flapping, Georgia resolved to march out there and face Carter, putting any attraction she might feel in its proper perspective. Stress. That's all it was.

Georgia threw open the bathroom door to find Carter reclining on an air mattress he'd set up for himself on the floor next to the bed. Again, the stress reared its ugly head and she found herself reacting to the new and improved Biggles-Vanderhousen boy. *Wow.* He was wearing a pair of old gray sweatpants and that was it. Nothing else. Not socks, not a T-shirt, not glasses.

He glanced up from something he was reading and smiled. "Hi."

"Hi." She pointed at the twin air mattress that was now

sitting atop a white linen sheet that he'd draped over the frame of the waterbed. A down sleeping bag and pillow were already set up for her convenience. "Is that mine?"

"Yeah. I sprayed some disinfectant on the frame and cleaned it up as best I could. I found a pile of roach traps in the closet and set them all around so we should be good for tonight."

"Oh. Thanks."

"No problem. You find everything you need in your bag?"

She nodded. "Pretty much."

Tiptoeing around Carter's bed, she made it to her own just as the room began to vibrate. Again, the light fixtures trembled and the sounds of distant thunder built, causing the tiny hairs at the back of her neck to stand on end. Before she could contemplate her motives, she dove from her mattress onto Carter's and scrambled into his lap. Like a small child, she looped her arms around his neck and buried her face in his shoulder.

When the train had passed and quiet reigned again, Georgia reared back and peeked up at Carter. "I'm sorry. I feel like a real goon. It's just that the train is so loud and it sounds like—"

Carter brought his finger to her lips. "I know. It's okay. Really."

"I'm, uh, just going to get back into my own bed now."

"Good idea."

Clumsily Georgia clambered off his body and slipped into her sleeping bag, still trying to reconcile the hunk on the floor with the kid from school. In the eerie silence that ensued after she snapped off the nightstand lamp, her thoughts traveled back to the old days, back at Hidden Valley elementary.

Carter was always a brain. Always daydreaming. Never

really fit in. After she'd moved to Oklahoma, she'd never thought of him, unless her mother mentioned something after a phone conversation with Daisy. In fact, last she'd heard, he'd gone off to school to study something or other, and that was that. She'd assumed that he'd simply faded into the woodwork in some company's lab as the resident genius and was glued to a microscope and growing moss under his feet.

She blinked down at him through the moonlight that filtered in through the crack in the drapes. Not so. Carter was hardly your typical scientist. He was more of a…he was sort of…he was…what was he?

*"Psst."* She wondered if Carter was still awake.

"Mmm?"

"Cootie Biggles, just who the hell are you?"

Carter chuckled. "I'm still the same kid you knew in school. Just taller."

"Bull."

"Okay, so I drive a cool car."

"I'm never going to go to sleep with all those roaches running around, so you might as well entertain me."

"Ah. You don't have to worry about the roaches. The rats will eat 'em."

Georgia burrowed under her bag and tightened the string around her neck. "Gee, thanks. Now I'll never sleep again."

"Okay, ya big wuss. I'll entertain you. Where do you want me to start?"

"The beginning is generally useful," she quoted, and she could fairly hear him grin.

"Well, let's see. After you moved away, I studied hard and graduated with honors from high school before my sixteenth birthday."

"That doesn't surprise me."

"In college, I earned an accelerated degree in biotechnology and law from Texas Technical University."

"That doesn't surprise me, either." She could hear his covers rustling as he turned on his side, propped his head on his arm and made himself comfortable.

"From Texas Tech, I headed to Central European University for my master's—and graduated summa cum laude—in political science. No brag, just fact."

"Not surprised."

"After that, it was on to The Bard Center for Environmental Policy where I studied in the Master's International Program in Collaboration with the Peace Corps. Then, because I was homesick for, uh, the South, I guess you could say, I ended up in Oklahoma at the U of O Health Sciences Center, working on a duel Ph.D/M.D. program in biochemistry and molecular biology."

"Wow."

"It was fun."

"Oh, it sounds like a blast."

Carter laughed.

"Then what?"

"Well, one time, when I was in Saudi Arabia on business for my dad, I started thinking about an idea that could lead to perpetual motion. The more I thought about it, the more I knew I had to see if I could make it work. Not only to protect my own family's legacy, but also to protect the earth from air pollution, acid rain and global warming and, worst-case scenario, another world war."

Georgia curled on her side and smiled. "That's mighty nice of you, Cootie."

"Thank you, ma'am."

She stifled a yawn. "So then what?"

"You're sure I'm not keeping you up?"

"Just talk."

"Well, that's when I decided to start up my little company."

"And what do you call this little company again?"

"CBV Research, Incorporated."

"Ohh. Sounds official." Suddenly boiling, Georgia battled her way out of her sleeping bag and sat up. She had to select her misery. It was either the heat or the rats. Sweating, she decided to stay cool until something drove her back into her bag.

"Yep. It's official."

"So." She dragged her hand through her hair. "What do you research, exactly? Give me the Dick-and-Jane version, please, as I only have a BS in business and *that* took me five years."

"Okay." Carter rolled onto his back and stretched his arms up over his head. "Basically, what we've invented is a small encoded chip that would help the car develop its own power. The best example I can think of is a waterwheel."

"Why not just use a waterwheel?"

"Wet. Messy. Big, big car, like a swimming pool with wheels."

Georgia hooted. "How cool! Kids would love it."

"Not practical."

"Yeah, I can imagine parallel parking would be a toughie."

"Not to mention driving on hills." They laughed for a moment, then Carter continued. "And here's the rub. With a waterwheel, the wheel drives the pump, which pumps the water back up to a holding tank and then it flows to the wheel again. But this only works in theory."

"Why?"

"Because it takes more energy to pump the water back up than the wheel can produce. That's what perpetual motion would be, if the wheel could somehow produce the energy needed. If somebody could do that, the wheel could run forever and never need fuel."

"And you have."

"No."

"No?" Crossing her legs beneath her, Georgia scooted toward the edge of her bed and peered over at Carter. "Then what on earth are we running away from? Why would someone kidnap Brandon over something that doesn't exist?"

"Well, we may not be there yet, but we're close. With our technology, the car could develop most of its own power. Not all. But most."

Deep in thought, Georgia propped her chin in her hands. "Oh."

"And most people think that cars like this have to be devoid of style. Not true. You rode here in one today."

"You're kidding."

"No."

"Wow."

"Yeah, wow." In the darkness, Georgia heard Carter push himself upright. "You know what? We forgot to eat. You hungry?"

"Come to think of it, I'm starved."

"Marshall packed us a boatload of MREs and some snacks."

"What's an MRE?"

"Meals ready to eat. The military and the space program use 'em all the time. You have a craving for anything? Soup? Mac and cheese? Some kind of freeze-dried mess that will come to life with water in my hot pot?"

"Anything. I could eat the hot pot." Georgia reached over and snapped on the bedside light as Carter dragged the food duffel up onto his bed. Within minutes he had several pouches of food simmering in the hot pot.

"Tonight's entrée is chicken à la king."

"Sounds fancy."

"Doesn't taste that way, but it's better than nothing. Here." He handed her a paper plate filled with a steaming pile of some noodle-like stuff and a plastic fork jammed into the middle. For a long moment they sat in silence, devouring their meals. When they'd finished, Carter made cups of decaf coffee and passed Georgia a dinner mint.

"Mmm. Just like the finest restaurant." She held her foam cup to her lips. "This has been so enjoyable, I'm considering moving here to Toad Suck."

Carter lifted his own cup. "To Toad Suck."

"To Toad Suck."

And with that the carpet began to vibrate.

# Chapter Six

At the crack of dawn, Carter woke Georgia from a deep, languorous sleep. The touch of his hand on her arm had her smiling dreamily up at him, her eyes at half-mast.

"Hi."

She exhaled through her nose, and lifted her arms above her head in a gesture that made her look vulnerable and girlish and, as far as Carter was concerned, quite irresistible. Her cheeks were smooth, her eyes clear and her lips rosy and kissable. A yearning built, deep in his heart, to perch on the edge of the bed and run a hand through her hair. To kiss those lips until she was fully awake. But he had to remind himself for the umpteenth time, her allegiance was to Brandon.

For now.

"Come on, sleepyhead," he whispered, "it's time to go. We can never stay in one place too long."

"Mmm. Don't we want to check out first?"

"No. She's got my card number. We'll just leave the keys on the table."

He reached to the foot of the bed and tossed her a pair of sweatpants. "Here. Put these on for now. I have everything packed and ready to go, except for your bedding."

Pushing herself upright, she looked him over, taking in his jeans, T-shirt and tennis shoes. "You look fresh and well rested. The dark circles are gone from under your eyes."

"I slept well, too."

"How long have you been up?"

"Half hour."

"That is *so* not fair. You're fresh as a daisy. I want a shower. To wake up."

"No time now. Besides, you look beautiful."

She glanced at her hands, her smile suddenly shy. "Man, I must have totally passed out. I didn't think I'd sleep at all."

"We had a busy day yesterday."

With a groan Georgia threw back the covers and swung her legs over the edge of the bed. "Busy? Is that your word for terror?" She rubbed her hands over her face and mouth. "I could sleep another few hours."

"Can't. Gotta get going."

"Where are we going now?"

"Another motel not too far from here." Carter slid his sunglasses on and gave them a jaunty tap. "I have directions and reservations.

"Oh, joy. I hope it's half as nice as this place."

He issued a snort through his smirk. "There is hot coffee and a granola bar waiting for you as soon as you're ready to go."

"Okay, gimme a minute." Groggily, Georgia stumbled to the bathroom to do her business while he deflated and loaded her bed.

Moments later she found Carter waiting for her in the car, engine growling. After she'd buckled up, he handed her a cup of scalding coffee.

"Mmm. Ambrosia. Thanks." She blew at the steam that rose from her paper cup. "Have you heard any news this morning about Brandon?"

Carter took a slug of his own coffee. "Yeah." He nodded. "Just got off the phone with Marshall at the local FBI headquarters. First of all, I learned a little bit more about this Rocky character. His full name is Reginald Klondike. He owns a failing oil operation, just south of Hidden Valley and has been relying on the sketchy cattle market to keep his business afloat. The Feds have been looking for this Klondike character for over a year in connection with several unsolved cases. One case, in particular, involves the murder of a senator."

Eyes wide, Georgia broke a chunk of foam off the edge of her cup with her teeth, then blew it away. "You're kidding."

"I wish. At any rate, Marshall tells me that Klondike— and the guys he was hanging out with at the party—are the prime suspects in Brandon's disappearance."

"They took him because he was trying to make them think he was the phantom, huh?"

"Yeah. Even if he wasn't the phantom, they probably figured he has information that will take them to the real thing."

Georgia dropped her head back in the seat and wailed. "*Ohhh, craaap.* This is all my fault."

"No, it's not. If I'd kept *my* mouth shut, none of us would be in this predicament now." Carter's jaw worked as he slipped on his special dark glasses. "I knew better than to even allude to the subject. Especially at a party where I suspected they might show."

"Yes, but *I* was the one who repeated what you told me—"

"Look, we can sit here and bicker over which of us is to blame, or we can get out there and find Brandon."

"You're right." Her face took on an expression of steely resolve. "Let's go."

Carter put the car into gear and rolled out onto the road. The sun was just peeking over the horizon, and already people were out and about, getting on with the banality of life, unaware of the drama that played out in the sleek black coupe that purred past. After several minutes of silence Georgia finally pointed at the ashtray. "Can we at least call Big Daddy?"

"He already knows you're with me."

"Oh." She cast him a quizzical glance. "And he's okay with that?"

"Yeah. That surprises you?"

"Kinda. I guess."

"Why?"

"Because Big Daddy is very protective of all of us girls. He doesn't trust just anyone."

"And what about you?"

"You're growin' on me."

Carter grinned.

As they pulled into the minuscule burg of Boring, Texas—population 683 and the site of their next motel—Carter contacted Marshall for further instructions.

"We're here."

"Good. Check in and lay low."

"Easy for you to say. You don't have to fend off the bugs in these places."

"They're not gonna look for a Brubaker in just any old

dump. Anyway, you really need to stay inside. Keep Georgia out of sight. Since our last conversation, we have new information leading us to believe these guys are actively looking for her now."

"I figured as much myself, but I don't feel it's really necessary to stay holed up in this—" Carter pulled into the motel's parking lot and stared in disgust at the shabby building "—dump till you round up these guys and haul them all in. Give me something to do."

"Not this time, Carter. We're setting up a complex sting operation and have decided it's best for you to be patient and wait out the time. Since you have the woman with you, your job is to concentrate on keeping her safe."

"But…"

"No. Lay low. That's an order. We'll contact you just as soon as we know anything."

Carter reared back in agitation as the dial tone sounded over the speakerphone. He pinched the bridge of his nose between his thumb and forefinger and rubbed for a moment. His smile held the insincerity of frustration. "You heard the man."

"Do you mean to tell me that we're just going to sit here and wait for them to find Brandon?"

"You know…? No." As if making a sudden decision, Carter slipped on his dark glasses and consulted the map in his e-zone. "All right. According to this, there's a campground about a day's drive from here in a little place called Haines Junction. Says it's near a lake. It's in the opposite direction than we are supposed to be traveling. And best of all, according to my calculations, it's very near Rocky's hometown and better yet, his property. You game?"

Georgia held up her hand for a high five. "I like the way you think, Carter Biggles-Vanderhousen."

He slapped her hand, threw the car into gear and, rubber burning, headed out of Boring and straight into adventure.

As the miles passed, Georgia and Carter went over every detail of the party conversation. Tongue protruding, pencil and pad in hand, Georgia tallied up as much detail as she could remember.

"Okay, so far we know that Rocky, aka Reginald Klondike, said, and I'm paraphrasing here, 'We can't have this maggot—'"

"Hey, now."

"'—eating our livelihood out from under us. If he succeeds in mass marketing this "alternative" fuel, we'll eventually be out of business.' And then, he said, let's see…" She tapped her pencil against her chin.

Carter glanced at her and pulled his smile between his lips. She was really getting into this amateur detective stuff.

"For motive, I'm writing, 'Must stay in business.' Okay?"

His nod was solemn. "Check."

"Good. What we don't know for sure yet is if they've figured out Brandon is not the phantom they've been hunting, which leads us—" she scribbled "—to the sixty-four-thousand-dollar question. What will they do with Brandon when they figure that out?"

"Probably hold him for a ransom they have yet to announce."

"And that will be…me?"

Carter glanced at her, but said nothing.

"Okay. Me. Makes sense."

"We need to change your appearance."

"We do? How?"

"Radical plastic surgery."

"What?"

"Kidding."

"Funny."

"I was thinking you could dye your hair, change the style of your clothing and makeup. Stuff like that. You need to be someone else for a while."

"That's fine. But who?"

"I don't know. You do any kind of accents or anything?"

Deep in thought, Georgia pressed her lips together and hummed. "I can do this garage-band-groupie-with-an-at-titude thing that makes my sisters laugh."

"That's perfect. Goes with my hair. So what's our story?"

"You mean, who are we?"

"Yeah. Where do we come from, why are we together, where are we headed, why...you know, the stuff people might ask us while we're out snooping around."

"Ooo. Fun." Excited, Georgia squirmed around in her seat to face Carter and, after pawing through the drink holder, found a pack of gum. She unwrapped two sticks and stuffed one into her mouth. "I want my name to be Fuchsia."

"Sorry, Marshall furnished us with new ID, and you are Lori Sanders. I'm your hubby Keith. But I guess I could call you Fuchsia as a pet name. Although, I'm more of a 'honey' kind of guy." He winked.

"Whatever." Georgia colored and waved a dismissive hand. "Anyway, I'm originally from Akron, Ohio, and I'm a surfer."

"A surfer from Akron, *Ohio?*"

"Yeah, sure, why not?" Giggling, she held the second piece of gum up to Carter.

"Because your ID says you're from Boise, Idaho."

"I wanna be from Akron."

"Fine. Be from Akron. I'll be from Boise." Carter lipped the stick into his mouth and could almost swear his lips vibrated where her fingers pushed the last bit in. He stole a quick glance at her as she sat, straining against the seatbelt.

Brubaker dimples in full bloom, she made furious notes. "And we are traveling across the United States to California to be professional surfers on the Extreme Sports cable TV show because that's where the big bucks are."

"Do you even know how to surf?"

"No. Do you?"

"No. Do you know anything about the sport?"

"No. But I saw a few Gidget movies when I was a kid." Carter lifted a shoulder and gave his gum a thoughtful chew. "Okay, I guess that will have to suffice."

"I think our motivation should be that we are in search of the ultimate wave."

"Great. What about us? Keith and Lori 'Fuchsia' Sanders. How did we meet?"

"Hmm." Georgia picked up her pencil and gnawed on the eraser. "I think we should stick close to the truth because it's easier to remember that way. Let's just say we met in grade school. That we were high school sweethearts."

"Oh yeah, like *that's* the truth."

"It could have happened." She cracked her gum between her back teeth and Carter could smell the mint on her breath.

"Oookay. I'm from Boise and you're from Akron and we went to *what* high school?"

"Uh…Performing Arts?"

"How am I supposed to keep a straight face with this kooky story?" he wondered, and Georgia was laughing too hard to answer. He rolled his eyes and grinned. "What'd we do, run away to get married?"

"Sure. Say we got married in Vegas and got turned around in Nevada on our way to California."

"And ended up in Texas?" Carter dropped his head back and shouted with laughter. "We *are* a couple of complete idiots."

"Fools in love." Georgia grinned. "We don't want to look too smart, do we?"

"I'll concede that point. We're gonna need costumes. If we're going to be idiots, we should probably look like idiots."

"Okay, I'll dye my hair. Fuchsia and, um, black and some other colors. And I'll do some heavy makeup and I'll wear like a bathing suit with a raincoat and army boots."

Carter's lip curled. "Yum. Now there's my woman. I guess I'll need a surfboard. And we'll need a different set of wheels. This thing will attract too much attention."

"And pink hair won't?"

"Yeah, but the car would attract the wrong kind of attention. We need an old van or something. We can get that when we get to Haines Junction."

"Ahh. Good idea. We could camp in it that way."

"That's true."

Then, just realizing what they'd committed to, they exchanged awkward glances. "Or—" Georgia shrugged "—we could get a couple of tents."

"And we're on our honeymoon? We *are* a couple of idiots."

They laughed for a good mile.

That afternoon, they found a picnic table at a roadside park where they could spread the Chinese takeout they'd bought from a place called Sneaky Pete's Chili and Chinese. While they were eating, they put the finishing touches on their story and began to work out the rough beginnings of a plan to locate Rocky and from there, Brandon.

"I think you should call me 'babes.'"

"Sounds juvenile. Sure. Babes." With a roguish grin, Carter swirled a chopstick in her direction. "What are you going to call me?"

"I think I should call you Cootie."

"Aw, c'mon." He exhaled in disgust. "That's not very sexy. Think of something else."

"Sexy, huh? Okay, how about 'cutie'?"

Carter snorted around a mouthful of fried rice and mumbled, "Now that we know who we are and where we are going, we need to come up with a way to execute a logical plan for finding Brandon." He waved at a bug with his napkin while Georgia made notes. "You gonna eat the rest of your barbecued pork?"

Absently Georgia pushed the carton in his direction. "No, you can have it."

Carter stabbed her pork with a chopstick. "You're sure you remembered and wrote down everything that Rocky and the men at the party said. You didn't leave anything out."

"Don't think so." Georgia flipped through her notes then grew thoughtful. "You know, I've kind of avoided thinking about the part where they started talking about his mobile butchering unit. That was pretty creepy."

"Why?"

"Because it upset all the guys that were there. I mean, Carter you should have heard him talking. He was very…sinister. You don't think he might have been talking about—" Georgia nibbled on the eraser end of her pencil "—butchering a person? After all, one of the men made it sound like he'd done it before."

"Klondike runs cattle on his oil fields, right?"

Georgia shrugged. "True. A lot of folks do. My family always has."

"Then he would probably be set up to butcher. From the sound of it, he can move around with a mobile unit."

"Yeah. A lot of folks do that, too."

"Do you think he'd butcher cattle for other people?"

"No doubt. Sounded to me like he's got money problems."

"Then write this down. Part one of our plan is where we have Rocky butcher our cattle."

"What cattle?"

"Well now, that's where 'the plan' comes in."

"What plan?"

"I don't know yet." Carter dug two fortune cookies out of the take-out bag and tossed one at Georgia. "Maybe the answer is in here. You have to say 'in bed' after you read it."

Georgia broke open her cookie. "Why?"

"It's funny."

She shrugged and focused on her fortune. "Okay. 'Never kick a fresh turd on a hot day' in bed."

"What?" Carter twisted her wrist around and stared at the fine print. "What the hell kind of fortune is that?"

"I don't know. What do you expect from a joint like Sneaky Pete's Chili and Chinese? Read yours."

He stared with misgiving at his cookie before he broke it open and pulled out the slip of paper. "'Never smack a man who's chewin' tobacco.'"

"In bed," Georgia reminded him. "You know, I really don't get that 'in bed' thing."

"Yeah, well, you'd need a real fortune cookie, I guess."

As they tooled down the main street of the quaint, all-American Haines Junction, they passed a used-car dealership that had one decrepit-looking van parked off in the corner by itself.

"Oh, my gosh, Carter slow down." Georgia bounced in

her seat and pointed out the window. "Look at that van! It's perfect! And the sign in the window says it's only five hundred dollars!" She unsnapped her seat belt and practically crawled over his lap. "Look! Over there. It's all rusted out, peace signs and flowers painted all over it, I love it!"

His nose in her shiny blond hair, Carter inhaled then shook his head and nudged her back into her seat. "Yeah, but does it run?"

"Who cares? It's so...so...*us!* It just screams Lori and Keith!"

"I'm beginning to feel like something out of the Partridge family."

"C'mon, get happy," Georgia warbled as they slowly cruised past. "Oh, I love it, Coo! You have to buy it for me. As a wedding gift."

Unable to resist her enthusiasm, Carter pulled around the corner and parked at the curb in back of the car dealership. They piled out of the car, stretched their cramped limbs, adjusted their clothes, locked the doors and headed through the lot toward the ancient VW van.

"Now let me do all the talking."

Georgia snorted. "Why? You think I don't know how?"

"You know how to talk, yeah. How many cars have you bought?"

"None. So?"

"So, I have. I'll talk."

No one was around, and the door was open, so they climbed inside the van to have a look around. It smelled of musty carpet, incense, smoke and the little pine tree air freshener that hung from the rearview mirror. One window had been broken and repaired with several layers of duct tape, and the interior walls were warped with age. There were only two bucket seats—driver and passenger—the other seats had been removed and the floor carpeted, most likely for use as living space over a quarter century ago.

"Oh, man," Carter breathed. "Check it out, babes."

"I love these black-light posters! And look, Coo! A lava lamp!"

"This was somebody's make-out den, huh?" Carter turned around in the tight compartment and began to inspect the cupboards.

Georgia snooped on the other side. "Look, a little plastic disc to plug in your pony keg and keep it cold and everything. And, see, a tiny sink and cupboards and an eight-track tape player. Oh, we have to have this!"

"Looks like it's in pretty good condition."

"Totally hip for a couple of hipsters like Keith and Lori Sanders."

Behind them, there came the sound of a man clearing his voice. They jumped, then laughed. Carter got out of the van first, and then turned and helped Georgia down. He grasped the hand that was proffered and shook.

"I see you two are interested in this vintage van. Yessiree, Bob, they don't make 'em like this anymore. A regular rolling love nest. Needs a bit of tuning, but runs like a dream." The portly salesman slipped his thumbs under his suspenders and rocked back on his heels. "And all for an unbelievably low price."

Georgia's enthusiasm could not be contained. "It's just perfect! We'll tak—"

"It's true. My wife here—" Carter slipped his arm around Georgia and yanked her up close "—and I are on our honeymoon and we're in the market for a...er...nest. But we're on a budget."

"Well you're in luck, cuz this one's handsome and the price is right at only six hundred dollars."

"Too much. Would you take two hundred cash?"

"Sold." With a resounding snap of his suspenders, the salesman led them into his office to get started on the paperwork.

## Chapter Seven

Gripping the massive steering wheel until her knuckles glowed white, Georgia sputter-putted down the road after Carter in their new VW "luv-nest" as the salesman had insisted on referring to their purchase.

"Yep, she'll make a fine little luv-nest for a young, honeymooning couple like y'all. Git ya one o' them blow-up mattresses and you're all set for a regular luv-fest in the luv-nest." A deep chortle had rocked his body as he had slapped the tabletop at his clever innuendo.

Once they'd signed the last of the papers, they'd unloaded everything that wasn't hardwired into Carter's car and loaded it into the van.

And then they were off.

Striking out on their quest to find Brandon.

First stop, ditching Carter's car. Georgia had no idea where they were headed exactly, as Carter had said he'd know the perfect spot to hide his car when he saw it. Al-

ready the challenge of keeping up with him on the highway, when the luv-nest would only top out at thirty-five
mph with the pedal to the metal, was giving her a tension
headache. On the main street alone, she'd been the victim
of more than one rude gesture and some pretty vicious cat-
calling as she tried to keep her tortoise behind Carter's
hare. Though the salesman had assured them the van was
in "Jim dandy" condition, Georgia had to wonder just how
long the poor throbbing engine would last. Carter seemed
to think he could handle any problems the old girl coughed
up, and she found a certain amount of comfort in that.

Finally—blessedly—he turned off the main highway
and headed down a gravel road toward a cluster of foothills. Georgia followed him for a good five miles before
he turned onto what looked more like a horse trail than a
road. After another mile they arrived at a grove of trees
shading a fairly dense thicket. There, an abundance of tumbleweed had collected. Without regard for the car's beautiful black surface, Carter plunged into the undergrowth
until all that Georgia could see of him were his taillights.

And then, nothing.

She jumped when he yanked open her door and nudged
her over.

"Should be safe here," Carter said as he adjusted the
VW's mirrors to accommodate his height.

"Are you sure? I mean, what if someone finds it and
steals it?"

"They won't get far. It's filled with tracking devices. Besides, who would look for a car out here in the middle of
thousands of acres filled with scrub brush and tumbleweed?"

Georgia surveyed the horizon. Nothing but puffy white
clouds in endless blue sky and tumbleweed traveling at the
mercy of the winds.

Kind of like them, she mused, then sighed. "Nobody, I guess."

"Right." Shifting the van into Reverse, he gunned the engine and tossed her an agreeable wink. "C'mon. We gotta get back to town and to the store for some shopping. Then we have to make it to the campground and check in before the ranger station closes for the night."

"Yeah, well, good luck making any kind of respectable time in this old girl. I'm afraid she's not exactly built for high-speed chases."

"That's okay. The lake is not far from here."

On the way back to Haines Junction, Georgia made up a shopping list of supplies they'd need for the next few days. When they'd arrived at the small grocery and camping supply store just outside town, Carter parked the van out front. The sign promised live bait, fishing licenses and ice-cold beer.

A cowbell jangled as Carter pushed open the door. Refrigerated air and the various smells of rubber, rotisserie hot dogs and wood polish greeted them as they stepped inside.

"I'll handle the groceries," Georgia suggested as she picked up a plastic shopping basket. "You get all the other stuff."

Carter agreed and disappeared down the hunting aisle.

Taking her time, Georgia meandered along, perusing every shelf for items on her list. This store only offered a handful of hair dye colors. All of them were a brand she'd never heard of, all of them way beyond their expiration date and none of them pink. For pink hair, she figured she'd have to resort to the package of markers she found on the office supply shelf. The makeup section was sketchy, as well, so she figured the markers would come in handy on that note, too. When she'd sorted out the hair problem and made her selection, she gathered what other toiletries she thought might come in handy—hair spray, extra shavers, sunscreen and the like—then headed to the aisle that offered some entertainment.

The paperback book and magazine choices were pretty much limited to topics such as *Fly-fishing Made Simple* and *Motocross Monthly*. She picked up the one passable novel, a half a dozen candy bars, various foodstuffs not included in Carter's larder, bottled water to drink and several packs of playing cards.

She lugged her booty up to the cashier station, but when no one appeared to ring up her purchases, she left her basket on the counter and set off to find Carter. He was in the back of the store with the clerk, listening to the benefits of "this here shotgun, over thut other." At their feet it seemed Carter had built a purchase pile of his own: a camp stove, a tank of propane, a tarp, waterproof matches, batteries, kerosene lamps, all manner of fishing gear—including a container of dirt and wiggling worms—several boxes of shotgun shells.

"Bullets, darling? On our honeymoon?"

"Babes, you never know when a quality shotgun will come in handy." He squinted down the barrel, taking aim at a giant elk's head mounted over the back counter. Uncanny. He really looked like he knew what he was doing. Still, just because he could handle a gun like a pro didn't mean she felt good about carrying a weapon.

"But, Coo…" she protested.

"Babes." His glare silenced her. "We'll take the shells. And a couple of fishing licenses, too. I already have an old shotgun. This one's a beauty, though, some other time."

Moments later they had stored their booty in the back of the van and were on their way.

"There wasn't much in the way of surfer apparel in there," Georgia said.

"Yeah, they cater more to the redneck."

"Okay. So far we are going to show up at the Klondike place as a couple of surfers with your old shotgun and ask him to butcher our nonexistent cattle while we snoop around for Brandon. Think he'll suspect anything?"

"There's more to the plan. I just need to think on it some."

Georgia groaned. "What should we do for clothes?"

"We could find a thrift shop, or maybe—"

"Or—" Georgia pointed down the street at a neon sign tacked to a telephone pole "—maybe we could go there. Huge yard sale."

"Where?" Carter pulled over so that she could better read the sign.

"Fifth and Oak." She squinted at the smaller print. "Okay, it says it's an all-neighborhood sale, today only…baby furniture, books, kitchen appliances and *clothes!*"

The yard sale was, as promised, a neighborhood affair, spanning the entire length of Oak Street. Seemed that all of Haines Junction had shown up to get in on the end-of-summer deals. Parking spots at the curbs were all filled, and hordes of people were picking through boxes and card tables and various display units, hoping to find that perfect treasure before someone beat them to it.

Georgia had hopped out of the car before Carter was completely parked and headed for a rack of brightly colored clothes. He let her shop for a while and wandered around on his own, poking about the various garages and yards with an eye out for anything that would aid them in their costuming. When he caught up to her, he couldn't keep the broad smile off his face.

"You're not gonna believe this!"

"What?" So engrossed was she in sorting the clothes table, she didn't look up.

"A surfboard. Check it out."

"No way." Georgia glanced at the board. "Wow! Who'd have thought?"

"I know! Haines Junction, for crying in the night. The guy who owns it says his son used to vacation in Cancún. Had a bunch of like-new scuba stuff, too, but I passed on that." He eyed her growing pile. "Look at you. You've been busy. You go to these kind of sales often?"

"Never."

"You really look like you know what you're doing."

"Well, that's because I do. Shopping is shopping. You're either good at it—" she held a miniskirt up to her waist and stared down at it, deep in thought "—or…you're not."

Carter scratched his head. "Actually, I'm not." He set the surfboard down. "This was just dumb luck."

"Don't worry. I've already found a couple of things for you to try on. The dressing rooms are set up in that garage over there. Here." She handed him a fistful of sleeveless, tie-died shirts and a pair of giant cargo shorts appropriate to their new surfer-dude lifestyle. "Go try these on, then meet me back here when you're done."

As she watched him walk away, Georgia exhaled the huge breath she'd been holding. She'd known he easily could have tried the shirts on out here, but somehow the mere thought of watching his stomach ripple as he lifted his arms over his head, set the guilt to stabbing at her brain. They were here to find Brandon. Not off on some teeny-bopper honeymoon.

While Carter was gone, Georgia pawed through the merchandise and found a box that was, for her, a jackpot.

Carter returned with the clothes. "They fit. Except for the pants. You can see my underwear."

"Good. Then they fit, too." She took them from him, stuffed them in the box she cradled against her chest and muttered, "We are so in luck."

"Why?"

"The owner's daughter just left for college. Check this out." She dug through the box and held up a chunky, lace-up, knee-high boot and a cloth bag of hair do-dads and costume jewelry.

Carter peered into the jewelry bag and pulled out an ugly ring with a giant shiny oval stone in the center. "Of what rare—and completely ugly—gemstone is this little number made?"

She took the ring from him and slipped it on her finger. "It's not a gemstone, silly, it's a mood ring. How square are you?"

"Ah. So, what mood are you in?"

Georgia pursed her lips and stared thoughtfully at the ring's changing colors. "As I recall, this light blue color signifies that I'm very smart."

"Smart is not a mood."

"Is so."

"Okay. Fine. Now it's turning a violet pink. As I recall—" he paused and stroked his chin "—I think that means you want me."

Georgia blanched. Did it show? "I'm so sure—" she snorted to hide her mortification "—it does not mean I want you."

"Yes, it does. And look, your cheeks are turning violet red to match."

"Are not."

"Are, too." Carter reached for her hand and pulled the

unattractive knob off her thumb and slipped it onto his little finger. "Lets see what mood I'm in."

Georgia bent her head over his hand. "Yup. Mmm-hmm. Just as I suspected. You are stupid."

"No. No, that's not it. I think you need to see it in a different light. Here. Come over here behind this tree, and you'll see what I mean." Taking her by the wrist, he led her behind the trunk of a giant oak tree, and dropped to one knee.

Georgia huffed at his silly antics. What in thunder was he up to now? They were going to run out of daylight, and then he'd be sorry. Besides, the owners were going to think they were trying to rip them off. Skip off without paying, even if the total bill only came to a few dollars.

"What are you doing?"

The afternoon sun filtered through the leaves of the oak's canopy, lending a dappled quality to the orange-gold light. A soft breeze sighed through the branches, and suddenly Georgia felt her heart pick up speed. Her breath came in herky-jerky spurts. Her heart seemed to understand before her mind could register the meaning behind his actions. "Carter?"

He took the box from her arms and set it at her feet. She stared at the box, and when he didn't delve inside, gazed quizzically into his eyes. She swallowed at the depth of emotion she found in his otherwise ordinary expression.

"I'm writing another chapter to our story. You know, so that when we tell people how I proposed, it will seem real." He slipped the ring off his pinkie and held it up between his thumb and forefinger. "Georgia Brubaker Lori Fuchsia Sanders Babes—" he swallowed, hard "—I love you. Will you marry me?"

Georgia stood and stared at him, her mind whirling with questions that she could never ask. Certainly Carter Biggles-Vanderhousen was not really proposing to her, Georgia Brubaker. Was he?

Good heavens. That would be ridiculous. Wouldn't it? After all, even though she spent the first eight years of her life with him, she hadn't seen him for years. He certainly wasn't trying to imply any kind of message with this little prank. Was he?

So, knowing he was teasing, she did her best to keep her tone light when she returned his penetrating stare and stated, "Yes, Keith. I love you, too. I'd be proud to be your wife."

She was kidding. Wasn't she?

As she looked back into the past, Georgia felt a smile steal across her lips and into her heart. Visions of the boy and man began to blur and meld into one. He was still brilliant. Still tender-hearted. Still getting into trouble.

Yep. She could easily fall for him. The timid child, the adventurous man and all the colors of the spectrum that lay between. She wasn't one to believe in love at first sight. All that gobbledegook about fate and soul mates and that stuff had never really been her bag. Until now. Now she was beginning to think there might be something to Shakespeare's star-crossed-lovers theory.

Yet, Georgia knew, as Carter took her hand in his, she could hardly do anything about that now.

Not until they found Brandon.

As Carter slipped the silly ring on Georgia's ring finger, it seemed to somehow begin to glow. They both stared at it, in that magical light that preceded twilight, mesmerized. Lifting their eyes, they looked at each other and smiled. It was a powerful moment. Nothing was said aloud, but with every beat of their hearts it was becoming clear that genuine feelings were pulsing to life.

Slowly Carter stood and murmured. "With this ring, I thee wed."

Deciding to play this game for all it was worth, Georgia glanced around and spontaneously rushed to get a hula hoop from a table mounded with toys. Returning, she dropped the hoop around Carter's neck and whispered, "And, with this ring, I thee wed." Using the plastic hoop, she pulled him close.

He bent to rest his forehead against hers. "For better or worse," he said.

"For richer or poorer," she said. "In sickness and in health."

"Forsaking all others, until death should part us."

Their eyes slid closed.

"Life is really short, huh, Carter." Thoughts of the danger for Brandon flitted through her head bringing with it fingers of anxiety. Thoughts of the danger into which they were entering caused those fingers to squeeze.

"Yeah," he whispered and then brushed a light kiss over her lips. "Life is far too short, Mrs. Sanders. Far, far too short."

Carter lifted the hula hoop between their faces, and then let it drop back down to encircle them both. Georgia clutched the plastic circle at their waists and smiled up at him. It was amazing. The vows they'd spoken had an odd effect she hadn't expected. The crazy image of them taking these vows before God and her family suddenly flashed through her mind. If they lived that long, of course.

Impossibly, her smile grew until she knew she must look as besotted as she was beginning to feel. "You may now kiss the bride," she whispered.

His answering smile held a promise that shimmered between them before he slowly, and with great deliberation, took her face in both hands. Tipping her chin with his thumbs, he leaned forward and lightly settled his mouth on hers. The kiss was exquisite. Soft, slow, gentle. His fingertips caressed her temples and then her jaw. All the while his lips feathered over hers, coaxing, teasing but never demanding.

The fact that he didn't exert any pressure—but just seemed to hover, reveling in the sensation of their combined energy—drove Georgia nearly mad with the need to clutch him closer. To escalate the kiss. But she didn't. Instead she endured her impatience and found that in denying herself, she found the sensations increased tenfold.

For all she was worth, she held on to the hula hoop, glad for its support at her lower back, as her body had become as boneless as a lazy cat. Once again, Georgia found herself *in* the moment, oblivious to her surroundings.

"So, you two want me to add the hula hoop to your pile of clothes?" the woman whose daughter was off to college inquired politely. "We're getting ready to start shutting down here, so if you have more shopping to do, now would be the time."

"Yes." Wobbly on her feet, Georgia sprang back as far as the hoop would allow and tried to act as if there was nothing unusual about the passion they'd stopped to express in the middle of her yard sale. "Yes, we'll take this pile here." She gestured to the box at her feet. "And that surfboard over there."

"Fine." The woman picked up Georgia's box. "I'll have this waiting for you at the till when you are done…uh, shopping."

Georgia was still sorting through their booty as Carter pulled into a gas station and got in line. "I can't believe they had all these really great eight-track tapes. I'm so glad I found them before we left."

"And us with an eight-track tape player." Carter slapped his forehead with his palm. "How cool is that?"

"Shut up. You're gonna eat your words when I crank the Stones. And look, they even had this old Boston Pops tape. Brandon loved that kind of stuff."

"Seriously?"

"Yeah. Brandon had this really huge music collection and we were listening to it when…" Georgia's voice trailed off and her expression became shadowed.

"Stop feeling guilty."

"But I—" she gave her head a tiny shake "—I…" She swallowed.

"Guilt won't get us to him any faster."

"I know."

"Marshall and Zach are the best. They'll find him soon, if we don't get to him first. It hasn't been all that long, so, please—" Carter reached out and stroked her cheek with the back of his hand "—try not to worry."

Georgia sighed and pressed his hand between her cheek and shoulder. "I'll try."


Hoping to make wise use of her time, Georgia decided to dye her hair while Carter pumped their gas and then paid for it inside the tiny minimart. After a moment spent searching through plastic shopping bags she finally located her box of Jet Brunette hair color. Having never dabbled with color herself, this was a brand-new experience, and not one she felt altogether confident in performing. Then again, this was no time to worry about her looks. Brandon was out there somewhere, and he needed Mrs. Lori Sanders to come to his rescue.

Funny—she mused as she tucked a towel around her neck—how she'd come to be the one rescuing Brandon with Carter's help. And she'd feared it would be the other way around and she and Brandon would be spending the week attempting to save Carter from himself.

After she tore the top off the box and fished out the directions, she unfolded the paper—now yellowed with age—and began to sort out the procedures.

"'Caution. Hair color products can cause' bla, bla, bla 'and, in certain rare cases, can be serious and lead to cessation of upper respiratory function, and in certain laboratory animals, coronary thrombosis, liver failure and precancerous tumors. Avoid contact with eyes. Use of this product on eyelashes may cause blindness.'" Georgia blinked at the parchment she held in her hands. "Good night nurse." Some guttural laughter burbled forth. "Surely they can't be serious."

Unafraid, she snapped on the enclosed rubber glove. "Brandon," she mumbled as she found the bottle of developer and snapped the top off with her teeth, "I gladly risk my life for you." She spat out the plastic nub, rubbed the horrible taste from her tongue with her neck towel and began reading the rest of the directions.

"'Using the enclosed utensil,' bla-bla-bla—" Georgia waved her free hand and muttered under her breath as her eyes scanned the fine print. "'Ratio should be one part' bla-bla-bla 'to one and one-half parts' yada yada yada. 'Apply to test area, let dry, wait forty-eight hours…' *forty-eight hours?* What?" She looked into the tiny rearview mirror and frowned. "Forget that." She glanced out the window. Carter was putting the gas cap back on the tank. She was running out of time here.

"Okay." Georgia shrugged. She was young and healthy and would no doubt come through a little hair-coloring session with flying colors. Her little pun had her chuckling.

"Here goes nothing." Using the provided plastic cup, she squeezed in the toothpaste-style developer, added a chunk of color and stirred up the reeking Jet Brunette mess. It had the oddest lumps swimming in the bubbly mess. No matter what she tried, they wouldn't break apart and, in fact, seemed to…grow. She gave the directions another glance over. Nothing about lumps.

Hmm.

*Man.* They weren't kidding. The fumes in this stuff were powerful. Her eyes burned and she had to fight back the tears that suddenly welled up. This stuff was thicker than she thought it should be. The consistency of…well, tar. Only thicker. And lumpier. Again, she blinked over the directions. Nothing about consistency.

And it was definitely black.

In light of the time crunch, Georgia decided to forgo her worries and began to smear the mixture directly into her hair.

"Whoo! This stuff is stah-*rong!* Phew, baby." As it did when she ate ice cream, a headache came on with sudden intensity and stabbed her right between the eyes. She was starting to feel a little dizzy. Her nasal passages felt as if she'd stuck a hot poker up her nose, and her throat contracted. Coughing, Georgia suddenly began to understand the manufacturer's respiratory concerns.

Bravely she continued to massage the color into her hair with her gloved hand. She glanced into the cup. Good grief. She'd used the whole box of this stuff, but it was nowhere near covering all of her hair. A big patch on the top of her head was pretty well covered in black tar, but it wasn't working out to the blond ends no matter how hard she smeared and massaged.

"Ohh, man." Her eyes were on fire. She could no longer

read the fine print. Was this one of the signs of blindness the directions had promised?

No, no. Of course not.

Okay. Wiping her eyes with the gloved hand, bad idea. Her eyes were melting. Damn. She'd forgotten to check how long she was supposed to leave this stuff on. With her nongloved hand, she slapped at the stinging spots she'd just rubbed into her eyelids. With the gloved hand, she tried to roll one of the van's windows down. Too bad they all seemed to be duct-taped shut.

Have mercy.

The fumes were growing. Swirling. Choking. Horrible. Certainly turning her poor liver to Swiss cheese with every burning breath she drew. Her heart was pounding and she began to feel faint. Coronary thrombosis was setting in. Eyes tightly shut, she patted the area around her until she found the directions. Tears rolled down her cheeks. Her nose ran. The pain in her eyes made her want to scream.

Georgia held her breath and, blinking rapidly, strained to find the 800 number for kidney failure.

*Precauciones: Los productos detintes para ell cabello puden causar una...*

She blinked and rubbed and hyperventilated some more. She had to get out of here.

Water.

Yes. That would help. She emptied her water bottle over the top of her head and then rubbed at the water-repellant Jet Brunette goop with her neck towel.

"Carter!" She pounded at the window, hoping to draw his attention. "Carter!" She strained to hear. No answer. Had the product caused her to go deaf, as well? No. She was simply panicking. *"Carter!"*

Okay. Time to take matters into her own hands. Groping blindly, Georgia found her way into the driver's seat, fumbled for the door handle and managed after several vain attempts to open the door and roll out. Hands outstretched sleepwalker style, Georgia stumbled onto the pavement and headed to where she'd remembered seeing the rest rooms, when they'd first pulled in.

Georgia felt along the exterior wall until she came to the doorknob of the ladies' room.

At least she thought it was the ladies' room.

"Georgia?" There was a note of dread in Carter's voice. A note that said she looked like hell. A note that said he was certain she'd been attacked by Rocky and the gang.

A note that said she'd walked in on him in the men's room.

# *Chapter Eight*

Once Georgia convinced Carter that she wasn't dying, but merely having an extreme hair day, he rushed her outside and hosed her down in the car wash area. Gasping and squealing like a kid in the sprinkler, she flailed about under the icy blast and fought the stream of water that would occasionally catch her in the mouth, causing her to choke and sputter.

"Georgia! You have to stop fighting me! Stand still!"

"Ouch! *Coo*—" she took a swing at him "—you are drowning me!"

"Listen. You can't see. We have to get that stuff out of your eyes before it does some real damage."

Remembering the package label, Georgia stood still and let him clamp his hand around her head and shower the stinging tar out of her hair and eyes. And, she had to admit, though the water was a shock, it did take her mind off the pain. After rinsing away every last drop of Jet Brunette, Carter tossed the hose aside, stripped off his shirt and used it as a towel. She had to clutch his arms as he vigorously rubbed her face and head down, to keep from toppling over. Finally the burning seemed to abate and she was able to breathe a little easier.

Until she opened her eyes.

Then, her throat closed all over again.

*Heavens to mergatroid,* The more opportunity she had to study his naked physique, the more impressed she became. She sucked in a lungful of air. He was truly a work of art. Something a sculptor like Michelangelo might have carved from granite. Smooth and hard and possessing a quiet strength that caused a deep yearning in the pit of her belly. She had to clap her hands over her eyes to keep from reaching out to touch this masterpiece.

Why did he bring out these feelings in her?

"Still hurts?" His voice was filled with sympathy.

"Yeah. You could say that." Only, she knew she wasn't referring to her eyes.

"What went wrong?"

"The box said it expired before the turn of the century."

"This century?"

"Ha."

"And you used it anyway?"

"I needed a new look. It was all I had."

He snorted. "Here, let me see."

Before she could protest, he gently pried her hands from her eyes and, tilting her head back, inspected each one for damage. The concern ebbed from his expression and his gaze slowly traveled her face. "Mmm. Yep. Just as I suspected."

"What?"

"They're beautiful."

"Yeah, if you like that bloodshot hound look."

"Love it."

He pressed a light kiss against one eyelid and then the other. "All better."

Georgia stood there, eyes closed, swaying in a nonexistent breeze. "Um, yeah."

"Good. Why don't you go put on something dry. I will, too. When you come out, the van will be parked over there—" he pointed "—by that phone booth."

Georgia stared into the ladies' room mirror, agog at what jet-black hair with hot pink streaks at the sides could do for her image.

It was incredible.

At first she'd been horrified over the spotty, mangy look that the Jet Brunette dye had given her silky blond hair. But once she'd filled in the blank spots with markers, it didn't look all that bad. Didn't look all that good...but, hey.

She was an extreme kind of gal now.

Luckily this hair dye was temporary and should eventually wash out. She pushed the button on the hand dryer, bent over at the waist and shook her head like a wet dog. After her hair was completely dry, she fastened in some of the rhinestone hair clips she'd bought at the garage sale and, using the sketchy supplies she'd assembled, applied a coat of makeup with the heavy hand of a teenager. Then she pulled a miniskirt, a tube top and the pair of horrible army-style boots from her bag and quickly dressed.

Lips pressed together, she stood back and surveyed her work.

Yeah. Georgia Brubaker no longer existed. In her place stood Mrs. Fuchsia Lori Sanders. Babes. Wife. Surfer.

An idiot on a mission.

Searching for the big wave.

And Brandon.

Donning her new bright red sunglasses with the rhine-stone-studded arms, she stepped out into the sunshine, a new creature.

"Holy galoshes, Batman." Carter could only stand there and stare, as Georgia emerged from the bathroom and sauntered toward the van.

"Hey, Coo," she called, and gave her hair a little fluff. "You look pretty phat, yourself." She looked over his garb and gave a low whistle of appreciation.

He felt like a complete fool, standing there in the shorts that drooped off his hips, gaudy flip-flops and the skintight, sleeveless shirt, but as long as he looked nothing like the Carter Biggles-Vanderhousen at the Brubaker party, he guessed it was worth it. To better hide the fact that he was gawking at her, Carter slipped on his shades. It was so hard to believe that she was even the same person. Only her voice was recognizable. Somehow she'd managed to combine the looks of Cleopatra, Sid Vicious and—he swallowed—an angel.

"Unbelievable." He gave his head a tiny shake.

"Yeah, Keith, you, too. They'll never recognize us now, huh?" She yanked open the passenger door and climbed aboard. Carter's heart swelled as he stood there and grinned for a moment. She was giving this mission 110 percent, just as she had back in the old days on the playground. Always ready to jump into the fray and champion the underdog, no matter what was required of her.

What a woman.

As she struggled to don the old-fashioned seat belt, Carter tried to, and couldn't, pinpoint exactly what he liked about Georgia's new look, except for the fact that under all that kooky clothing and makeup, it was still just Georgia. He loved the way she looked. Blond. Jet Brunette. Pink.

He simply loved Georgia. Her enthusiasm. Her eagerness to participate. Her willingness to accept life as it came to her, without setting herself apart. In all his years of searching around the globe, he'd never met another woman that could compare.

He doubted he ever would.

"Okay. I think we should call Rocky and make an appointment to have our cow slaughtered," Carter said as he guided the old VW down the road. They were headed for the Haines Lake campground, where he'd made a reservation while he waited for Georgia to finish dressing. The sun was setting and long shadows were unfurling across the landscape.

"Okay, what cow?"

"The one we'll worry about later."

"Right. You want me to call him now?"

"Yep." Carter handed Georgia his cell phone. "Dial 411 and have 'em connect you."

"Do you think we should try during the dinner hour?"

"Think Rocky keeps regular hours?"

"Probably not." Georgia's nose wrinkled as she dialed. "What should I say if he answers?"

"Just say we heard through a friend of a friend that he might butcher a cow for us. Ask him how much he charges, when he could fit us in, stuff like that."

Georgia held the phone out to him. "Why don't you do it?"

"Fuchsia, you're a Brubaker. You can do it. I don't think they'll suspect a woman caller as much as they—"

She waved at him to be quiet as the operator came on the line. "Haines Junction, Texas. Reginald Klondike. Please."

Carter continued to coach in a whisper. "Remember, you are Lori Sanders, extreme surfer."

She nodded and listened as the phone rang at the other end. A man picked up on the third ring.

"So, okay, like, hi. Yo, is like there a Mr. Reginald Klondike there, or what?" Georgia pulled her chin back into her neck and bunched her shoulders and shot Carter a hapless look. "You are Reggie? Oh, sorry, Rocky? Klondike? Oh. Cool. Well, like the reason I'm calling is because like I have this cow? And even though I'm a vegetarian, I'm into organic meat, and like she's the only cow I trust not to kill me from pesticides and hormones and junk, if I like, ya know, eat her and stuff."

Carter stared at her and mouthed, "Too much information."

She cocked her head and sent him a shut-up-and-let-me-handle-this look with narrowed eyes. "So, I was wondering if I brought my, uh, my Bernadette by, if you guys could like b-b-butcher her and…and…chop her up and get her freezer-ready for me."

Georgia listened to the voice on the other line.

"Cash. Yes. How much? Okay, fine. Tomorrow afternoon? Already? Uh, two. Sure, okay, that's cool." She scribbled some furious directions. "Right. Uh-huh. Okay. We'll be there. Thanks. Bye." She pushed the Off button and looked up at Carter. "We need a cow."

As Carter maneuvered the van into their reserved RV spot, the camping community eyed them with suspicion. People looked up from magazines, paused in lighting the barbecue, and peered out tent flaps for a better look at the new kids on the block. The expressions on their faces were similar and without words seemed to scream:

"What's with the surfboard, here at the lake?"

"What's with the pink hair?"

"You're not gonna rob us or anything, are you?"

Sensing the fear and animosity, Georgia stretched her lips into a huge smile and waved at everyone as she jumped out to help Carter guide the van into position.

"Hello." She peered into the neighboring space where an elderly woman and her husband stared at them with apprehension.

"I'm Lori Sanders. And this—" she pointed Carter out as he cut the rumbling engine and set the brake "—is my husband, Keith. We're from Akron and we're on our honeymoon. We eloped. In Vegas. Didn't win any money, as you can see." She laughed. "But we have each other and that's all that matters to us. Right, honey?"

Carter flashed them a peace sign. "Right, babes."

"Anyway, like I was saying, we just got married in Vegas, and for our honeymoon, we're headed to California for the big wave, cuz we want to try our hand at professional surfing and stuff before all the babies start coming—"

The neighbors simply stood and stared.

Carter moved up behind her and massaged her neck. Her head dropped back and her eyes fell shut. "Isn't he wonderful?" Lazily she squinted at them. "Okay, where was I? Oh, right. We got a little bit turned around." She giggled. "I was driving while Keith was asleep, and well, he can sleep like the whole day away and so—" she giggled again "*what-ever.* Here we are. But that's no biggie because we have like our food and camping stuff. And Keith wants to kill at professional surfing on Cable TV for a few weeks, before we settle down, right honey?"

"Ohhhhh, yeah. Gonna ride the pipe."

"Yeah. Ride the pipe, Coo."

Suspicion faded and the older woman smiled. "Why, that's just what we did, huh, Ted?"

Ted sat, a literal bump on a log and grunted.

"I'm Mary, and this here—" the little pudding bag with the gray topknot explained as she clapped her husband on the back "—is my Ted. You kids kind of remind me of us when we were young. We didn't want to be surfers, of course. Ted wanted to travel the rodeo circuit and ride the big bulls. But in the end it's all the same, huh, kids? Have fun while you're young. That's what me and Ted always say, right Ted? And by golly, we're still havin' our fun."

Ted poked at his fire with a stick and issued an agreeable grunt.

As Carter slipped his arms around Georgia's waist, she settled back against his chest and suddenly believed with all her heart in everything she was saying to Mary. It seemed completely plausible that she and Carter were young and in love and running off into their future. Only in the details was reality lost.

As Mary filled them in on the bliss of a ripening union, Georgia looked with fond envy at the two raisin-like faces. Though old Ted wasn't much of a talker, it was easy to see that he loved Mary. Georgia tried to imagine a similar future with Brandon as her better half and couldn't.

But with Carter—she snuggled into the circle of his warm embrace as they listened to Mary drone on—she could imagine a full life. A life of excitement, common interests, a house bursting at the seams with clumsy, socially awkward, runny-nosed little babies that looked just like Carter had when he was very young. Oh. She clasped her hands around Carter's forearms and squeezed. It was such a sweet fantasy.

"—and you two can come over for dinner tonight! We're

having a cookout and a sing-along with some of the others we've met here. We'll introduce you kids around, won't we, Ted?"

Ted issued his standard grunt and nodded agreeably.

*What?* Georgia had been woolgathering about life as Mrs. Georgia Biggles-Vanderhousen. She glanced up at Carter's serene face for a clue on how to handle this little surprise.

Good heavens. There wasn't enough time for frivolity. They had work to do. Camp to set up. Plans to finalize. A Brandon to find. Cattle to purchase by two o'clock tomorrow afternoon.

They needed some serious alone time to get organized.

"Oh, well," Georgia stammered, "we don't want to imposition you."

"Why, it's no trouble at all! Our treat! We won't keep you out too late. Ted and I remember what it's like to be newly married. Don't we Ted?"

This time, a grin toyed with Ted's wide, pliant lips as he grunted.

"If this van's rockin' don't bother knockin'." Mary whapped Ted with the potholder she held and hooted. "Remember that Ted? Remember when we used to say that?"

Ted grunted.

"Okay enough of that nonsense. I was just going to fire up the barbecue. Everyone will be here in a half an hour. Why don't you two go set up camp and then come on over."

"Carter," Georgia hissed from between smiling lips, as they wrestled the surfboard off the roof of the van and then unloaded all of the camping gear they'd purchased and began to sort it out. "We don't really have time for a sing-along. Aren't we supposed to be looking for a cow for me to take over to the Klondikes at two tomorrow?"

"Yes." Ever unflappable, Carter propped his surfboard against their designated picnic table. "But a few rounds of 'Kumbaya' aren't going to kill us. And what better opportunity to hone the details of our story on people who don't know us from Adam? We can learn from our mistakes now, before we move in on Rocky tomorrow."

Georgia frowned. He did have a point.

"Besides, I'm starved. And from the smell of things, Mary is great with the barbecue."

Georgia glanced over at Mary who was busy piling meat on the grill. "Yeah. Me, too, actually."

"While we eat we can ask old Ted what he knows about buying cattle. He was a rodeo guy, right?"

"According to Mary."

The smell of the barbecue had Georgia's stomach rumbling as she and Carter pumped up their air mattresses and cleared a spot for them in the van.

It didn't take long for them to unpack their sparse belongings, sort out their food and toiletries. Georgia draped a few towels outside over the windshield, and closed the curtains in the back of the van to afford them some privacy later that evening. Carter organized his tracking equipment and checked his messages while she unfurled their sleeping bags at opposite ends of the twin mattress and plumped their pillows.

"Marshall knows we're not in Boring, and he's not too happy with me," Carter told her after he'd placed a couple of quick phone calls. "But I think he'll realize—"

Unfortunately, before Carter could fill her in on that, and the latest on Brandon's whereabouts, Mary yodeled, "*Yoohoo!*" to summon them, and an eclectic group of "neighbors," to supper.

As it turned out, the entire group of campers had managed to put aside their preconceptions about Keith and Lori, and were delighted to add some fresh faces to the mix. Everyone welcomed the Sanderses with enthusiasm and more than a little curiosity.

After some quick introductions, Mary encouraged everyone to, "Grab a plate before everything gets cold. After supper, we got dessert and camp songs. I hope you kids know how to play Charades."

Georgia's smile was weak. "I...don't." She turned and shot Carter a searing glance that said they couldn't play Charades *now*. Not while Brandon still needed rescuing. "How about you, Coo? You ever play Charades before?"

"Nope. Sounds like fun." Carter headed off to grab a plate and load it at the grill.

Clearly—Georgia thought, feeling just a tad churlish—his mind was on his stomach and not on apprehending criminals.

Mary noticed their exchange and loudly excused the newlyweds from having to play Charades, as they most likely had other, more interesting games to play.

Carter's roguish grin said it all, and good-natured laughter rippled among the neighbors and set the tone for the rest of the evening. Sensing his gaze from across the campfire, Georgia glanced up, and when their eyes met, her cheeks grew hot and her breathing, shallow. If he was only acting, he deserved some kind of award. The wolfish lift to his brow announced to everyone that he wanted her and, indeed, had husbandly plans for some alone time after dinner.

Once they had heaping plates settled on their laps and had sated the sharpest of their hunger pangs, they began to indulge in small talk with the "gang."

First, there were Donald and Barb. Donny, as he liked

to be called, was a self-proclaimed redneck who absolutely never stopped talking about hunting. Barb was an accomplished musician and boasted of the ability to play obscure instruments, most notably her squeezebox, which she played on and off throughout the evening. Also present were the thoroughly agreeable Evelyn and Jim, who hooted with hearty laughter at the end of every sentence, even if the subject strayed to topics that Georgia had never considered in a humorous light.

By far the most annoying couple there that evening were Dot and Otis. When Dot wasn't passing out her business cards and trying to sell Carter and Georgia myriad cleaning supplies and detergents, her husband Otis practiced his fledgling Spanish for fun. He'd listen to the conversational learning tapes over his headphones and responded to what he heard, despite the conversation around him.

"¡Hola! Me llamo es Otis. ¿Dónde está el cerveza?"

Mary waved her barbecue tongs over her shoulder. "Beer's in the cooler, Otis. Help yourself."

Despite the fact that this was the most eclectic group of folks Georgia had ever encountered, she found that she was enjoying the kooky evening; most especially, posing as Lori Sanders. Carter had been right. This was the perfect opportunity to practice telling their story and sharpen their chops as a married couple. Not once did anyone question their story's legitimacy, and somehow even Georgia began to believe that she was Lori. That she and her Keith were bound by the vows of holy matrimony. Everyone offered congratulations and toasted their new life together, heaping on the advice and regaling them with stories of their own early years.

Although, Georgia had to admit, there were some awkward pauses and perplexed glances when Carter announced that they were in the market for a cow and hoped to make their purchase first thing in the morning.

Ted scratched his head. "But we was under the impression that y'all were off to do some surfin'."

"We are. But, uh, the um, the surfer's *code*—" mind whirling for an explanation, Carter bought time by clearing his throat, "the code is—"

Georgia jumped in, when he faltered. "Yes, the surfer's *code* is—" she looped her hands in circles, as if in doing so, she could pull the idea from his mouth "—is…"

When she didn't continue Carter rolled his eyes and cleared his throat again.

"Don't tell me you're plannin' to take your cow surfin'?" Ted wondered.

Evelyn and Jim nearly fell over with laughter.

"Oh, no, no." Carter chuckled. "No, actually, the, er, the code of the extreme surfer is, uh, protein."

"Oh, yeah." Face bunched into a solemn wad, Georgia nodded. "That is so key. Protein. Essential. Right."

"Why don't you just go buy yourselves a hamburger? It's a lot less fuss than buyin' beef on the hoof, butcherin' it and then tryin' to keep it froze." Ted looked at Donny. "Ain't I right?"

"Oh, yeah, unless you want to talk deer huntin'. If that's the case—"

"Oh, no." Georgia leaned forward and spoke in a confidential tone. "We favor domestic pets."

"You're going to butcher your *pet?*" Evelyn and her husband stopped laughing.

Carter shrugged. "We like to *know* our meat, before we eat it."

"Totally," Georgia agreed. "Know it, and know it well."

"Ya didn't take much time to get to know them sausages." Mary's comment held a wry note as she slaved away over the smoking grill.

Carter grinned. "Sometimes it's an issue of trust."

"And good vibes," Georgia put in. "Stellar sausages, Mary."

"Thanks, hon."

"How will you take your new pet on your honeymoon?" Otis asked, finally speaking English.

"We have room in the back of our van?" Georgia glanced at Carter for affirmation.

"Yep. We have room. That'll have to do for now."

"Well, you'll really get to know her, that's for damn sure." Mary pulled a second pile of dripping bratwurst links off the fire and shook her head. "You kids today with all your concerns about the food you eat. Takes the fun out of life, if you ask me. Seconds are ready. Come and get 'em at your own risk."

Georgia tented her fingers under her chin, affecting a deeply philosophical pose. "I think you can sum up the Sanderses' belief system this way—"

Carter looked at her with interest.

"It is our belief that while we are in training, we will only eat beef. But, being former vegetarians, we don't want to strike an animal down in its prime. So, we're looking for a more…mature animal."

Ted was still scratching his balding pate. "You want mature meat? That just don't make no sense. Old beef is tough."

Georgia groped about for a response. "Tenderizer?"

Ted shrugged. "Course, I ain't gonna tell you kids what to do, so, if it's old beef ya want, I'll put a call into a guy I know by the name of Linus. Doesn't live too far from

Haines Junction. Has a couple of old flea-bitten bossies he uses to mow the lawn. Probably could be persuaded to part with one of the old girls. Give me your cell phone there, and I'll call him up."

After the fifth round of "Michael Row the Boat Ashore," Carter knew it was time for him to head for shore. Literally. Aside from the fact that the music was beginning to fossilize his poor brain, he felt a cool dip would cure a number of his current ailments. Off in the distance, the water gently lapped, beckoning. An owl hooted. The moon was nearly full and shimmered in a triangular path across the flat surface.

Bending low, he whispered to Georgia as she lay on an old blanket, her head propped comfortably on his lap.

"You about ready to call it a night?"

She lolled over onto her back and looked up at him in the glimmering firelight. Her flawless skin glowed golden, and her eyes sparkled with mischief. Lazily she stretched and lifted her hands to stroke his cheeks.

His heart leaped and began to race.

"I thought you'd never ask."

Oh, he wanted to kiss her. Bad. Right here. Right now. But that hardly seemed polite. Not in the middle of a resounding squeezebox solo of "Michael Row the Boat Ashore." "Good. Feel like going for a quick swim before bed?" He needed one now, more than ever.

"Um." She stretched again and locked her hands behind his neck. "That sounds wonderful. It's still pretty hot."

"Yeah." Carter wasn't referring to the weather. And he could tell by her smile that Georgia knew it.

# Chapter Nine

Cricket's song echoed over the glassy surface of the water and seemed to fill the cathedral of trees that surrounded them with music from another world. From their lazy vantage point—straddling the surfboard in the middle of the lake—Georgia and Carter listened to the discordant continuation of the sing-along, off in the distance. Ted and Mary's campfire was now but a pinprick of light among the woods and, from above, the campfires of the fairies sparkled across the endless night sky. Rings of water rippled occasionally as the catfish jumped, but other than those soft intrusions, they were alone in a world made of moonglow and sultry summer breezes.

Georgia sat atop the surfboard, legs crossed, elbows to knees, chin propped in her palms. Carter straddled the board facing her, and propelled them in a leisurely fashion by paddling his feet. Their mood was languid, and everything, including their murmured conversation seemed to be happening in wonderful slow motion.

Georgia had never experienced such a magical evening in all her life. It was as if all that was perfect had converged in this small spot and she'd been somehow transported from the mundane to the enchanted. Here she was, living out the exciting fairy tale that she'd always dreamed of, and with Carter B. Vanderhousen of all people, as her knight in shining armor. Amazingly, he was all that.

And more.

Her own personal Adonis, paddling her gondola.

Was this what her sisters had felt, earlier this summer when they'd fallen in love with Big Daddy's ranch hands? Everyone had been surprised by their choices, having expected them to find matches in their own social circle. Georgia certainly hadn't understood their marriages until now.

Had they been awakened from a long, deep sleep by a lover's kiss? Because for Georgia, that's what had happened. In the unlikely location of the Toad Suck Motel's lobby, no less.

She was alive. Electrified. Alert, for the first time in her entire life. And the man, sitting there before her, was the reason.

"Where are we going?" she whispered, afraid that raising her voice would break this delightful spell.

Carter's reply was soft. "I thought we'd follow the road to the moon." He gestured to the swath of light that angled off to the east.

"Perfect." A nearby splash attracted Georgia's attention. "Mermaid?"

He processed that from right to left brain, then slowly nodded. "Probably. Certainly not a catfish."

"Mmm. My mama used to fix that for us when we were

kids. It was one of the few things she would cook for herself. She'd give the kitchen staff the night off and everything."

"I always used to wish I was part of your family when I was a little boy."

"Really? Why?"

"Because there was always so much noise and laughter and happiness and—" he cocked his head and studied her face "—you."

Georgia ducked her head and trailed a hand in the water. "I never knew you felt that way. Were you lonely?"

"Yes. And no. I used my imagination a lot. That skill has come in handy as an adult."

"I used to wish I was an only child."

"You're kidding."

"No. I have such flamboyant siblings. Next to them I felt positively invisible. Still do, to a large extent. Until, of course, you came home and I was kidnapped by a spy."

Carter grinned.

"So, what was it like?"

"What?"

"Being an only child."

"It was both good and bad. My mother was aware that I was a sickly runt of a kid and always tried to make it up to me by babying me. Sometimes she smothered me. I think that's why I left home so early and spent so much time overseas. I needed to figure out who I was, apart from my parents."

"And just who are you, Cootie Biggles?"

He stared off at the horizon, deep in thought for a moment. "I'm Carter Biggles-Vanderhousen. Entrepreneur, inventor, world traveler, and these days I freelance for the FBI as Keith Sanders, idiotic surfer dude and your husband."

"Lucky you."

He reached out and lightly pinched her cheek. "It's a dirty job, but somebody has to do it."

"Keith, do you think our marriage will last as long as Ted and Mary's?" Mortified, the kooky question was out of her mouth before she'd given any serious thought to the impression she would be making on him. Luckily for her, Carter answered in the spirit it was asked.

"I like to think of the Sanderses as a forever kind of couple."

"Yeah. Me, too."

A wistful feeling settled over Georgia. She stared at, but didn't really see, the flicker of their campsite. Their neighbors' wobbly voices, accompanied alternately by Barb's mouth harp were still playing homage to a gamut of camp songs. "It must be wonderful to share your life with someone you've loved forever."

She could feel Carter shift his intense focus to her face. "I can think of nothing I'd like better."

Gooseflesh pulsed down her spine, and when Georgia lifted her lashes, her gaze telescoped into his with an impact so forceful, she felt as if she had suddenly caught the backlash of a tidal wave and was riding atop a pipeline that would change the course of her destiny. Never had a man affected her this way before, and Georgia's social circle included many powerful men. She froze, riveted to his pensive expression, and wondered if he felt this extraordinary connection as strongly as she did.

Blood roared like ocean surf in her ears. Her heart thundered, and her mouth went suddenly dry. Though the lake was glassy calm, she felt buffeted by the passion that seemed to course between them, and she clung to the edges of the surfboard.

A slow smile curled his lips, rendering her incapable of

breathing, and she had the eerie feeling that he could read her mind. Heat stung her cheeks as she considered the thoughts that had been flitting, rapid-fire, through her brain.

"It's late," he murmured.

"Mmm." Her heart was lodged in her throat, preventing a more coherent response.

"We should probably be heading back, before Mary starts to worry."

"Mmm."

"She didn't like the idea of us going for a swim so late at night. Thought it was dangerous."

"Dangerous."

Carter lifted a roguish brow and murmured, "Feel like you're in danger?"

"Yeah."

Danger of losing her marbles. Suddenly Georgia was insanely jealous of the girl who so adeptly had taught him to dance. What else had she taught him to do? Had she captured his heart? Did he still carry feelings for her?

Many long minutes passed as they sat in silence, simply staring into each other's eyes. Without speaking they managed to relay feelings that no words could ever express. Without touching, they strengthened a bond that had begun when they were children.

And slowly, without fear of the past, Georgia began to understand that right here lay the beginnings of her forever.

Eventually they made their way back to camp, languidly paddling with their hands and feet. They used the campfire and the sound of Barb's tom-toms as their beacon. When they reached the shore, they found the towels they'd left on the blanket with their shoes and rubbed each other down, teasing and horsing around for the benefit of the neighbors.

Or so they'd convinced each other.

"That you, Keith?" Mary warbled. "Lori?"

"Yep, it's us," Carter assured her. "Safe and sound. Say good-night, Lori."

"Good night, Lori." Georgia giggled.

"Linus called me back after some thinkin'," Ted called, peering over the campfire and into the shadows. "He says he'll sell ya his old bossy. We'll go get her first thing in the mornin'."

"Thanks, Ted. We'll take you out to breakfast."

Carter draped his arm around Georgia's shoulders, and they waved good-night to everyone as they headed to their van. Just before he handed her inside, Carter pulled Georgia close and kissed her until her breathing became labored.

"What was that for?" she whispered against his lips when her brain could form the words.

"Ted was watching. Remember, we're supposed to be on our honeymoon."

"Ohh. Yeah. Right."

"You'd probably better kiss me now, being the ardent bride and all."

"Is Ted still looking?"

Carter affected a very solemn expression. "Trust me, Georgia. We have to act our parts in order not to raise suspicion. If he's not looking now, he might look again."

Georgia dimpled, her eyes narrowed. "You're raising suspicion all right."

"Just shut up and kiss me."

"When did you get so boss—"

Georgia never got to finish her sentence.

It was cramped inside the old VW van, what with all of Carter's investigative equipment from his car, their camping gear and yard sale purchases. As she tried to maneuver around, getting ready for bed, there was just something about the close quarters, the wobbly air mattress and both of them trying to maintain a modicum of privacy that tickled Georgia's funny bone.

"How ya doin' over there, babes?"

"Don't look yet." She giggled as she tried to wrestle her dry pajamas up over her damp skin. "I'm still getting dressed."

"But, honey. We're married now. I can look. It's part of my husbandly duty."

Hunched over, Georgia hopped on one foot, bobbing about with the giddy, punch-drunk laughter brought on by exhaustion. "Duty? Golly, Keith, don't make it sound so romantic."

"Honey, if I was givin' you the duty, you wouldn't be able to think of anything but romance."

More breathless mirth pitched Georgia to and fro. "Oh, Cootie, I love it when you talk duty."

"I aim to please."

Her slap-happy hilarity increased in volume. "Good boy. In that case…hand me my hairbrush…and then get my, my, my socks, will ya? They're…in that little cupboard over the…pony keg thingee." Her contagious laughter consisted of one long, lilting giggle that spurred Carter into clown mode.

"How am I supposed to do that, when I might accidentally look at you?" Staring at the wall over her shoulder, Carter screwed his face into a ridiculous pout.

Bless his sweet heart. Georgia could tell Carter realized she was exhausted and scared of their morning mission and needing some lighthearted distraction. And for his valiant efforts to entertain, she fell just a little more deeply in love with this goofy nut. Eyes closed, arms outstretched, he began to stumble blindly about as he searched for her slippers.

Intermittent bursts of laughter made it hard for her to speak as she hopped and wriggled into her pajamas. "Just…throw everything at the sound…of my voice. *Woo-o-ooonce—*" She snorted and hopped and giggled and hooted and struggled for a sobriety that simply wouldn't come. "Once I'm dressed…we can start…working on the master…plan for tomorrow and…*p-p-practice* what I'll say when I'm—" nerves only increased her raucous laughter, "undercover at Rocky's."

"Talkin' 'bout goin' *und-a-cuvah at Rockae's!*" Carter mimicked.

The van started to rock and Georgia stopped laughing long enough to gasp as she frantically grabbed at the curtain rods, and tried to maintain her sketchy balance. "What are you doing?"

"If this van is rockin'—" Carter beat his chest, Tarzan style, and jumped up and down "—don't bother knockin'!"

Taking the curtains down with her, Georgia toppled over, screaming with glee as she went. In order to disentangle herself from the musty, sun-faded fabric, she flailed her feet and tried to talk to Carter between fits of belly laughter. "What the devil are you doing, ya big weirdo?"

Carter affected a somber expression. "This is my scientific way of ensuring that our planning session is not overheard by the enemy or snoopy neighbors."

"Are you crazy?"

*"Yeeesss!"* Carter roared and, throwing himself into a wild rendition of the hula, rocked the van even harder. *"Yeee-hawww!* If this don't keep people away, nuthin' will!"

Oh, her cheeks hurt from laughing. "What will Ted and Mary think?"

"Nothing they haven't thought up before."

She moaned and gasped for air. "Stop it, or I'll wet my jammies."

"Ride that wave!" Arms out like a surfer, Carter balanced on an invisible board and whipped his head around to stare at Georgia. Eyes crossed, teeth protruding, it was the best Austin Powers impersonation she'd ever seen. *"Yeah, bay-bee!"*

*"Ohhhh."* Georgia could only lie there like a wet noodle and laugh until she feared something deep in her gut had ruptured. Finally she threw a tennis shoe at him. "Quit it! I mean it. I'm gonna get mad."

His British accent was flawless. "I love it when you're mad! *Go mad, baby!"*

The van swayed. Georgia squealed. Carter dropped to his knees and joined her on the tangled pile of curtains.

And they rolled around together and laughed until the tears streamed down their cheeks.

"I'm hungry," Carter whispered. They'd been plotting out tomorrow's events for over an hour now.

"What? You ate, like, six hotdogs over at Mary's."

"So? I'm a growing boy. Us surfer dudes need sustenance. Dude does not live by surfing alone." Carter rubbed his eyes. "Besides, all this planning stuff wears me out."

"Okay." Georgia sat up and rummaged through the grocery cupboard. "How about some raisins and cheese crackers and a can of tomato juice?"

"Yum. But only if you join me."

Georgia tossed him a handful of prepackaged snacks and then fired off two cans of juice, football style. He fielded them easily, then reclined back on his pillow and began to eat.

Georgia tore into a box of raisins and leaned back against her own pillow at the opposite end of the mattress. "Carter?"

"Huh?"

"Why haven't you married?"

He shrugged. "Never found a girl who lived up to my expectations."

"Which are?"

"Hmm. Good question." He popped a cracker into his mouth and gave it a slow, thoughtful chew. He swallowed. "I guess I'm looking for an ideal that I formed when I was just a little boy."

"How little?"

"Three. Four. I don't remember." He kept his eyes downcast, so Georgia couldn't read the subtext of his words. "Bravery. Loyalty. Protective streak. Adventurous. Those are all biggies to me."

Georgia's pulse stuttered. When she was very little, she'd been all those things. A veritable freedom fighter. But that was back when they were children. That was before she allowed the world to close in on her and stuff her into a boring little box. Before she'd let fear be the magnifying glass through which she viewed all of her choices. Did Carter still see any of those qualities in her today?

The very thought of going in after Brandon tomorrow had her quaking in her slippers. Would she be able to pass muster with Carter all these years later as she once again attempted to rescue an underdog from the bullies? Bringing a can of diet soda to her lips, she took a long pull as she mulled over these issues.

She'd spent so many years erecting walls around her heart. Walls that would protect her from the sting of not living up to the grand accomplishments of her older siblings. She was one of the middle children in a family of nine. Nothing special, really. Not in comparison to a doctor and a veterinarian and a CEO and all of the other amazing careers and awards and accolades her siblings had achieved over the years.

Carter's voice pulled her from her musings.

"Besides. Until now the time has never been right for me to marry."

"Until…now?" Her eyes widened as she attempted to digest this offhand proclamation. He was back in the States. Was that what he meant? His parents were moving back to their ranch for a while, time to settle down. Was that what he meant?

He'd reunited with the brave and loyal Georgia of his childhood.

Was that what he meant?

Mouth suddenly dry, Georgia touched her tongue to her lips and, because she had no idea how to respond, she changed the subject. "How did you know that eventually, someone from this oil cartel thing would come after you?"

Carter crossed his feet at the ankles and, lying back against his pillow, rubbed his palms over his face and groaned. "Unfortunately, my business has been plagued by a series of highly suspect 'accidents' and fires that concern not only me, but the FBI and those who work for me."

"You're kidding."

"No. It's terrorism, plain and simple. People attempting to control by fear. And it happens somewhere in the world every single day. Even right here, in our own country. We can't let that affect our efforts to make headway in the fuel industry for our children. And their children."

Georgia could feel the fear rising and her high, squeaky

voice was a dead give-away. "How do you know they won't just blow you off the face of the earth?"

Lips pursed, brows knit, Carter shrugged. "We don't. We can only take precautions. For example, in this last year, we have taken my business underground and secreted our laboratories in unpopulated areas on foreign soil. But even so, Brandon's disappearance is just another sign in a long string, that a growing group of fanatics aims to put a stop to our research."

"Wow." The blood drained from Georgia's cheeks as she listened. "If Rocky truly is part of this bigger group, our plan to rescue Brandon tomorrow needs to be really good."

"It is."

"Really? Do you really believe that? Carter, there are only two of us. To me, we seem as idiotic as David facing off against Goliath."

"Don't worry. Our plan is solid and not as haphazard as it might seem on the surface."

"Well—" Georgia exhaled noisily, as if she could blow her fear away "—even so, I'm praying."

"Good." Carter picked up their notepad and a pencil. "It's never wise to be overconfident. While you're at it, put in a word for me."

"I will."

Once again, just for drill, they reviewed the timeline they'd been hammering out. Logistically, it would be tight.

The day would begin at the crack of dawn with a trip to Haines Junction to purchase their cow. Then they'd have to drop Ted back at camp and head for Rocky's place. After they'd roughed out that schedule, they did some role-playing and rehearsed various conversational scenarios Georgia might encounter when they arrived at Rocky's. When they'd exhausted that topic and finished their snack, they climbed into their sleeping bags and smiled across the mattress at each other.

"Big day tomorrow."

Carter glanced at his watch. "Big day today."

"It's that late already?"

"Yep. We need some shut-eye."

"I'll never sleep a wink, for thinking about this ridiculous plan. I just know something terrible is going to happen. I'll flub up and leave you out there twisting in the wind...."

"You worry too much. Remember, this is my job. I've been involved in operations like this to one degree or another, since college."

"Hmm. I know me." With her fists, she gave her pillow a plumping and rolled over on her side. "I'll never sleep."

As he got on his knees to reach the light and turn it out, Carter murmured, "Sure you will. Just shut your eyes and relax."

Georgia yawned. "Hey. You never did tell me what Marshall said on the phone, before dinner."

"So far, no sign of Brandon. They've been watching the Klondike ranch very closely and are in the process of infiltrating his inner circle, but will not be taking any action until they've had more time to investigate his part in the syndicate. Personally, I don't feel we have that luxury. Anyway, by the time they have clearance from above to move in, we should have this entire mess put to bed." He glanced over his shoulder and suddenly smiled.

Georgia's mouth was slack and the tiniest of girlie snores puffed at her cheeks.

Carter rocked back on his heels and watched for a very long moment and felt his chest expanding with a love so profound, his ribs ached. It was the true, man-to-woman, head-over-heels-in-love, walking-on-air stuff that he knew would plague him till the day he died.

Unless, of course, she loved him, too.

And for Carter, *that* was the mystery.

# *Chapter Ten*

Clarabella the cow—not nearly as attractive as her name would indicate in Georgia's opinion—bawled something fierce as they lumbered down the highway toward Rocky's place. The mangy old bossy stomped and snorted and limped around in the back of the VW van, seeming not at all pleased with her new owners or their plan to have her butchered.

"Hey, Carter?" Georgia had decided to ride in back, thinking it would soothe the revolting animal. Big mistake. For now, she was pretty much hemmed in between the cow's swollen belly, the van's sharp cupboards and the cow's clumsy, cloven hooves. To make matters worse, a veritable horde of flies had moved in with Clarabella and insisted upon using Georgia's face and arms as their airstrip.

"Huh?" His sunglasses shielded his eyes, but it seemed his gaze was glued to the road with such grim purpose, it was almost as if—by the intensity of his stare—he thought he could force more power out of the aging horses in the engine.

"I think old Clarabella here might have to go potty."

"Aaaand...you would like me to do *what* about that?"

"Pull over?"

"And risk losing her again? No way. One morning spent chasing her out of Barb and Donny's camper was enough. We owe Barb a new squeezebox, by the way. A one-of-a-kind antique jobber, signed by none other than Lawrence Welk himself."

Georgia sighed.

It was true.

It had been one hellish ordeal after another to load—and reload—the petrified bovine into the van that morning.

Directly after a big farm breakfast at the Little Pigs Breakfast and Lounge, Ted had taken them over to Linus's place to introduce them to their "pet-slash-protein." He'd issued some raspy laughter and elbowed Linus in the ribs.

In Georgia's mind, this was when their plan took a turn from the ridiculous, to the sublimely ridiculous.

Frozen with fear, the bony bovine had locked her legs up like so many military flagpoles and refused to budge, no matter how they all coaxed and cajoled and outright shouted. After discussing various scenarios with Ted and his buddy Linus, about how best to load her into the van, it was finally decided that they would back the van up against her side and tip her in. Unfortunately, Ted had misjudged the distance between the VW's crooked bumper and the cow's crooked shanks and she'd simply tipped over onto the ground. She lay on her side, legs still rigid with what would have appeared to be rigor mortis if the cowed cow hadn't been bellowing at the top of her lungs.

"Yee-aaap." Linus nodded. "She's got a touch of the arthritis. Can't bend like she used to. We're gonna have to pick her up."

Carter stared at the skinny little man. "She weighs half a ton if she weighs an ounce. How the hell are we gonna do that?"

"Forklift."

"You got a forklift?"

"No, but Floyd Greasy, up the road a piece, does. He'll come do it for a few extra bucks."

True to Linus's prediction, Floyd showed up about an hour later, and—after he'd scoped out the situation—figured it would be best to pick her up from behind and load her in headfirst.

Too bad Floyd hadn't figured on the ditch.

The forklift couldn't quite counterbalance Clarabella's weight, and when Floyd got her in the air and swung her around, his rear tires lifted off the ground and Clarabella slid into the ditch. On her back. Legs in the air, eyes rolled back in her head, still bellowing.

Floyd lifted the brim of his cap and scratched his head. "Ain't nuthin' I can do about her down there."

Carter exchanged looks of disbelief with Georgia. "So we're just going to leave her there?"

"Nah. A crane'll gitter up."

"You have a crane?"

"Nah. But Hal Burkett has one. He'll do it for a few extra bucks."

A crane, a bucket of grain, some carrots and salt lick chunks, over a dozen men from the greater Haines Junction area and seven hundred dollars later, Clarabella was loaded and road-ready. Seemed they only had to wait for Billy Simmons to weld the rear door back onto the VW—for a few extra bucks—after Hal had ripped it off with the crane.

The situation was no easier once they arrived back in camp to drop Ted off. Seemed the call of the wild trumpeted through Ted's open door, and, forgetting her arthritis, Clarabella bolted.

Over hill and dale, through tent and camper alike, Clarabella visited as many people as possible while AWOL. Finally a pup tent that got tangled in her hind legs slowed her progress just enough to put her back into captivity.

That was over an hour ago.

Now they were back on the road again, and headed off to save Brandon. And just in the nick of time. It was nearly 2:00 p.m. Although, if they continued to make good time, it would be a miracle.

Clarabella's extreme weight nearly flattened the van's rear tires and cut their top speed considerably. Not that Georgia cared. She was in no hurry to face Rocky. Trying to convince a mobster that she was serious about actually eating this poor, flea-bitten, mud-caked, manure-spangled excuse for a cow was not something she was relishing.

"But Carter, the poor thing is carsick...I think. She's burping something foul and her eyes are still rolling back in her head." Georgia bent forward and peered into the old girl's face.

"Clarabella? What is it, hon?" The cow's nostrils flared and, like twin blowholes, they exhaled a shower of slobbery wet goop that had Georgia recoiling with revulsion. *"Ewwww."* With the hem of her blouse, she mopped off her face.

Finally Carter turned off the main highway and headed down a gravel road toward a cluster of rather familiar looking foothills. A funny feeling of déjà vu came over Georgia, and she frowned and consulted the map. In all her life, she'd never spent any time out here in Haines Junction. So why did she feel as if she'd come this way before?

They bounced along for a good five jarring miles before Carter turned again, this time onto an extremely rough road. Gnawing at her lip as they jounced along, Georgia alternately peered at the map and then again out the window until it dawned on her. Carter had printed the wrong map. This was the way they'd come the other day to hide his car. Not the way to Rocky Klondike's place. Okay, okay. They simply needed to download the Klondike map.

"Carter? I think we've made a little boo-b—"

"Uh-oh."

Georgia glanced up, but her weary smile slowly faded as she recognized that certain look on his face. The look that said, hang on to your hat, something really weird is about to happen. He was peering into the rearview mirror.

"What?" she asked, dread crawling up her spine.

"I don't know for sure."

"What don't you know? Carter, you're giving me the creeps. I can't see your eyes through those stupid sunglasses. What are you saying?"

"Someone's been following us ever since we turned down this last stretch of road. Turn around. See that SUV?"

Georgia pushed Clarabella's head out of the way. "Yeah?" A veritable dust storm swirled out from under the SUV's tires. Someone was coming up behind them. Fast. A feeling of lightheadedness had her seeing sparks and black floating dots. Her knees were weak, her stomach upside down and she had to clutch Clarabella's crusty neck for support.

"Why are they driving so fast? What do they want?"

"I'm not sure yet."

Her breath came in short, dizzying pants. "Carter? I thought we were going to the Klondike farm?"

"We're on the Klondike farm."

"No, no, no. You're turned around. This is where—" Georgia screamed as a bullet whizzed past her head. The back window shattered to the floor. Clarabella bawled.

"I decided it would be safest to hide my car in Rocky's backyard. Figured he'd never find it there."

"Safe? You call this *safe?* Why didn't you tell me we were on the Klondike property?"

"Didn't want to scare you." Carter put the pedal to the metal, but it wasn't much good against the V-8 that jetted up behind them. Taking cover under Clarabella's belly, Georgia crawled back under the animal's tail and, using it as a lever, lifted herself up for a quick peek out the window. Guns. Long ones. Pointed at them. She recognized Rocky.

She began to hyperventilate.

"Carter! Okay. I think Mr. Klondike saw through our...our...harebrained scheme."

"Ya *think?*"

A spray of shotgun shot blasted the rear of the van and the spare tire exploded. Georgia shrieked and threw her arms over her head. More gunfire had the van swaying. Clarabella lifted her tail and gave vent to her anxiety. Georgia crawled back to the front end of the cow.

"Uh, Coo? I think we should just tell them we changed our minds and turn around and, uh, go to California. We can even take the cow."

"Don't worry. Once we make it to my car, we'll be fine."

Another bullet zinged through the van. Carter ducked low, but kept driving, lurching down the primitive, deeply rutted road as fast as the poor old van would go. Clarabella bawled as she tried to stay on her feet. Georgia clung to the animal's scrawny legs and screamed and prayed that the cow wouldn't slip and fall.

"Don't *worry?*" she shrieked for emphasis. "Are you *kidding?*"

"No. I've got everything under control."

"Carter, they're *shooting* at us! They are trying to *kill* Keith and Lori!"

Another shot rang out and the van veered crazily. "Georgia."

Georgia whimpered in a high, squeaky voice. *"What?"*

"Do you trust me?"

"Yes?"

"Good. Then do exactly as I say, no questions asked. Now, get down and stay down! No matter what happens, do *not* leave the van. Just let me handle Klondike. Got that?"

"I guess…"

"Georgia!"

"Okay. Yes. I got that."

"Good." The thugs behind them showered the back of the van with another spray of bullets.

"Uh, Carter?"

*"What?"* he hissed, the cords on his neck bulging from his efforts to navigate the van the tenth of a mile they needed to reach his car.

"I know this is probably not the time, but just in case they kill us, I just wanted to tell you something."

"You're right. This is not the time."

"But, Carter, I can't die without telling you!"

Unable to answer, Carter stood on the gas and steered the old van like a captain at a ship's wheel during a tornado.

"Anyway…" At this point, Georgia didn't really care if Carter was listening or not. She had to get this off her chest before she was gunned down and went to her reward, "I just wanted to tell you how sorry I am that I invited Bunny Boatright to my uncle's party."

"Don't be."

"Oh, Carter, you're just being nice."

"I'm not."

"At any rate, I had no right to put you into such an...*eeee*—" a bullet zinged by, and both she and Carter dodged and weaved "—awkward position. But, you see...*eeee*...invited...*eeee*...her because I was told that I had to...spend the week showing you around, and all I could think about was that you were still the little...*eeeeeeee*...uh, you know, goofy boy, that you used to be, and I didn't want to be bothered. Besides, all I could think about was Brandon, and oh, Carter..."

By now the tears were streaming down her cheeks. Georgia elbow-crawled on her belly to the front seat as gunfire sounded from immediately behind the van.

"Get *back!*" Carter shouted.

Georgia turned around and crawled back with Clarabella. *Ohhh.* There was no way that just the two of them could ever fight this battle. In mere seconds her entire snooze of a life flashed before her eyes. Soon there would be a story on the evening news:

Local oil empire heiress, Georgia Brubaker,
her ex-boyfriend, Brandon McGraw,
her childhood nemesis, Cootie Biggles,
and her decrepit cow, Clarabella, all
murdered by the mob.
Film at eleven.

Oh, Lord, have mercy, she sniffed as bullets pinged off the bumper. We can't do this alone. And just when I found him, and life...I'm losing them both.

Her entire body seemed to vibrate with fear. They didn't

have a chance. They were dead meat. This was it. The big trip to Glory Land. She'd reached the end. And at only twenty-five years old. As she sobbed with sorrow over all the woulda's, shoulda's and coulda's, Georgia continued her nervous blathering. Venting her soul. Confessing her sins.

"I haven't thought about Brandon—at least not the way I used to—since you kissed me back in Toad Suck. It just struck me like a bolt of lightning. The impossible had happened. With you, of all people. The boy next door. You were a peculiar little kid, yeah, and I wasn't all that keen on having to save your sorry butt every time I turned around, but now I see that going through all that torture as a kid is what makes you such a tough, virile, sexy man. And I know we haven't had a date, like a normal couple and everything, but I just have to tell you that...*eeee*...I really...*eeeeeee*..."

The van would go no further and lurched to a stop next to the thickly wooded area. Shouting came from behind, men's voices cursing, and the rumbling engine of the truck grew closer. Waves of ice and fire enveloped Georgia, and she pushed her head between her knees and fought to stay conscious. Her head buzzed. She couldn't breathe. Panic had killed her air supply, stopped her heart and rendered her limbs useless. A curiously cold sweat broke out on her face, her hands, her feet, and she was certain that she was about to lose her lunch.

Carter's door was jerked open and he was pulled out and onto the ground.

All the while, Georgia screamed. *"Nooooo!"*

Just before she crouched behind Carter's seat, between the cow and their camping gear, she caught a horrifying glimpse of Rocky as he hit Carter's jaw so hard, his sunglasses flew off.

Crazed fury consumed Georgia, and suddenly she was

back in preschool and the bullies were kicking sand in Cootie's face. The same feelings of indignation that fueled her preschool outrage rose to the surface in the form of a low growl in her throat. There was no way she was going to let a bunch of mean bullies beat up her man.

Spurred by a nearly inhuman ferocity, she scrabbled around behind her looking for a weapon and the first thing her hand landed upon was the empty box of Jet Brunette hair color. And, while it would make one heck of a weapon—if she could just get close enough to do their hair—she needed something that would really scare the crap out of these guys. Something deadly. Something like…her hand landed first on a fishing pole, and then on the stock of Carter's old shotgun.

"Yes," she whispered and yanked the gun out from under the canvas. Only problem was the one thing they'd forgotten to plan: teaching Georgia how to shoot.

*"Ahhh, shoot."* She stared at the box of shells and realized she didn't have a clue how to load the stupid thing. Fingers fumbling, lungs laboring, she decided that there was no time like the present to learn. Grasping the sliding pump, she pulled it back and peered into the chamber. Empty. Well, okay, she'd just fill it. She tore off the lid to the box with her teeth and grabbed a handful of yellow plastic tubes with metal tips. She'd grown up on a ranch. There was no doubt in her mind that these were shotgun shells and they slid into the chamber. Yellow end first, she guessed and shoved a shell into the chamber and cocked the pump. The sound of the deadly clicks were just as terrifying as they were in the movies, and Georgia had to force herself to breathe.

It was time to save her man. Gripping the gun, Georgia staggered to her feet, squeezed past Clarabella and, screaming like a banshee, pushed open Carter's door and leaped to the ground. Her eyes were wild and she could only hazard a guess that—what with her multicolored hair and the shocked look on the faces that stared at her—she looked just a tad crazy.

Good.

Levering the gun at Rocky, she tossed her head and shouted, "Let him go or I'll shoot." Behind her, Clarabella chose that moment to once again let freedom ring and, bellowing like a rodeo bull, crashed out of the van and headed for the sunset.

"Georgia! Don't be stupid! Get back." Lying face to the ground, Rocky's boot in the back of his head, Carter was still issuing orders. Georgia rolled her eyes. Typical male. What in thunder made him think he was in control of the situation from down there?

"Don't worry about her, Rocky. She's not gonna shoot you," one of Rocky's friends from the party said.

Rocky had the unmitigated gall to laugh. "Yeah. One of you guys grab the broad and stick her in the van. We can deal with her later." He frowned when nobody moved. "*Move! Now!* She's not gonna shoot."

"The *hell* I won't!" Georgia pointed the gun skyward. "You leave him alone, or…" teeth bared, she screamed, *"answer to me!"* For emphasis she pulled the trigger and miracle of miracle's, it fired. The blast was so deafening she feared her ears were bleeding, and the gun's ferocious kick knocked her off her feet. There was a terrible crunch as she landed on the ground, and at first she thought she'd broken her neck.

But in her peripheral vision, she could see it was only Carter's sunglasses.

She lay there, the breath knocked out of her.

*Ohhh, crap.* She hurt all over. Inside and out. Tears coursed from her eyes and into her ears.

She'd failed. Failed to save little Cootie. And big Carter. Failed to save Keith and Lori and failed to save herself. Failed to save the world from the inevitable wars to be fought in the future over oil.

Time warped, and Georgia felt as if she were moving in slow motion as she reached under her neck and pulled out the broken sunglasses. She clutched them tightly, as they were her dying connection with Carter.

Within the thicket under the trees, came the sound of an engine roaring to life. Slowly Georgia sat up and squinted into the brush. Sounded like Carter's car. She slipped on the glasses to cut the glare, and sure enough, it *was* Carter's car.

But who was driving it?

The distraction of the engine enabled Carter to pull Rocky's foot off the back of his head and drop him to the ground before his car burst out of the underbrush and began to build speed as it careened toward the stunned group. All of the men but Rocky—who was now in the middle of a knock-down-drag-out with Carter—dropped their weapons and began to run.

Watching them fight from a distance, Georgia began to scream. "Get him, Coo! Kick him where it counts!"

Mouth open she turned to see Carter's car barreling down on him as he wrestled with Rocky for control of his gun. "Car-*ter!*" she screamed, her voice slow and stretched and echoing in her head like a lion's roar. *"Lo-o-ok ou-ww-t! Your car!"* By the narrowest whisker, Carter managed to roll both himself and Rocky out of the car's path just before they were run over.

"Georgia!"

"What?"

"Don't look at me!"

"What?"

"Don't...look...at...me!"

"Why not?"

The car spun around and came after Carter and Rocky again.

"Because it will go *wherever* you *look!*"

*"What?"*

"The car goes to whatever vector your eye moves."

*"What?"*

Carter groaned. Again, like a toreador with a bull, he managed to roll himself and a terrified Rocky out of the way of his speeding car.

*"Look somewhere else!"* Carter grunted as he tackled Rocky to the ground and jerked his arms up behind his back.

*"Where?"*

"Anywhere but at *me!*"

Rattled, Georgia fastened her gaze on the men who were running across the field. And, to her utter amazement, the hi-tech whiz car followed. In fact, wherever she trained her gaze, the car would go. A heady feeling of power assailed her as she watched the men run this way and that. After a few moments of practice, Georgia was able to herd them, like so many sheep.

With a final Herculean effort, Carter managed to knock Rocky unconscious and then, lungs heaving from his effort, settled back to enjoy Georgia's handiwork.

Off in the distance a siren sounded and quickly increased in volume. Within moments Marshall and Zach roared up in a black sedan, leading a number of local squad cars and Federal agents in unmarked vehicles. Officials poured out of their cars, guns drawn and bullhorns blaring.

Marshall slapped a pair of handcuffs on Rocky's wrists, and Zach read him his rights. Then Marshall had a few private words with Carter. When they'd finished talking, Carter trotted over to Georgia and lifted the sunglasses from her face and handed them to Marshall.

Georgia fell into Carter's arms, shaking with relief. And fear. And suspicion.

"How?" She looked up at him through narrow eyes. "How did everyone know we'd be here?" With her head, Georgia indicated the swarm of FBI agents out in the middle of the field, currently arresting Rocky's cadre of buddies.

"I never go into a situation like this without backup, so I called Marshall just before we left and told him that you and I were going out to round up Brandon and if he wanted to make some arrests, to be waiting for a signal at the foot of the Klondike driveway."

"What did he say?"

"Being that you are a lady, I'll refrain from comment. But he wasn't surprised. We've worked together for years. Deep down, I think he knew I'd never let that much time pass before I went in."

"And so what was the signal?"

There was an unmistakable glimmer of pride in Carter's eyes as he leaned back and smiled into her face. "I'm pretty sure you set it off when you landed on my sunglasses. You were very brave. You know that, don't you?"

Groaning, Georgia allowed her head to thud against Carter's chest. "But we still haven't got what we came for. Brandon is still missing."

"Actually…" A strange look came over his face, and Georgia's heart clutched.

"What? Carter tell me! Is he all right? Is he…alive?"

"Oh, he's alive all right. At least for now." Carter glanced around, his eyes skimming everything but her face.

Again Georgia's knees went week and she clung to Carter's shirt. He was avoiding telling her something. Telling her that Brandon was dying. Hurt. Badly hurt. Perhaps even paralyzed. The backs of her eyes began to sting. It was all her fault.

One lone tear coursed down her cheek and she look up at Carter, filled with self-loathing. "Oh, Carter." She pressed her cheek into his chest and took comfort in the steady beat of his heart. "Please. You can tell me. How bad is it? How…long does he have?"

"Awww, *shoot*." Carter took Georgia by the hand and led her over to the woods and lifted her up onto a stump. "I think you should be sitting down for this."

Georgia softly wept into the palms of her hands and nodded.

"Okay." Carter took a huge breath and slowly let it out. "I guess the best way to do this is to just tell you like it is."

She hiccuped her agreement.

"Brandon was never kidnapped."

Georgia abruptly stopped crying. "What?" She stared up at Carter through bleary, shell-shocked eyes.

"Oh, we all thought he was. In fact, until just moments ago, I believed we were off to rescue him. But it seems—" Carter ran a hand behind his neck and attempted to rub the tension away "—it seems that he ran off with…with…Bunny Boatright."

"Bunny? And Brandon?"

"Yeah. Apparently, they had a lot in common, and while you were dancing with me, Brandon was unable to tell you that they decided to take a quick stroll through the conservatory. When they returned and couldn't find us, Brandon drove her home. They've been gone for all this time together."

Georgia began to shake.

"Oh, honey. I'm so sorry. I hope you're okay. I didn't want to be the one to tell you. I wanted to be the one…" The more he talked the harder she shook. Carter circled her shoulders with his arm. "Please, sweetheart. Don't cry. He wasn't the right man for you. Honest."

He hunkered down on bent knee and peered into her face. His eyes narrowed. Georgia wasn't crying. She was laughing. His grin grew and spread until he began to laugh, as well. For several minutes they held each other and laughed until they couldn't laugh any more.

Finally sated, they slid off the stump and to the ground and, side by side, lay there, panting up at the clouds and occasionally chuckling at the absurdity.

"But why are the Feds arresting Rocky?"

"Apparently, even though he had nothing to do with Brandon's disappearance, he is a prime suspect in the murder of a senator. He's got a rap sheet as long as your arm and what you overheard at your aunt's party was all Marshall needed to reopen the case. Plus, he did shoot at us."

Georgia sighed. "Oh, I'm so glad. About everything."

"Now aren't you happy you invited Bunny to your party?"

Head lolling to better see him, Georgia sent Carter a blissful smile. "Mmm-hmm."

Carter reached for her hand. "So I take it there are no hard feelings between you and Brandon?"

Georgia slowly shook her head. "Just relief. Relief that he is safe. Relief that Bunny found someone nice. Relief that I don't have to worry about letting him down gently."

"Letting him down?"

"Yep." Georgia rolled onto her side. "I started to tell you in the van, but we—" she gestured to Rocky as a policeman assisted him into the back seat of a squad car "—were interrupted."

"True. So. What did you want to tell me?"

Their eyes clung for a long, meaningful moment before she spoke. "I wanted to tell you that I love you, Carter Biggles-Vanderhousen. With all my heart. And that the time I have spent with you has overshadowed any experience I have ever had in my entire life. Bar none."

A very slow smile of ecstasy crawled over Carter's mouth. "Same," he whispered. "I love you, too, Georgia Brubaker. And I always have."

He leaned forward just a tad and pressed his lips to hers. "This probably isn't the most romantic setting for this question, but I have to ask it, as I have wondered the answer since I was three years old."

Georgia grinned. "Fire."

"Will you marry me?"

"Oh, yeah, baby." She looped her arms around his neck and pulled him close for another kiss. "Ohhhh, yeah."

# *Epilogue*

*One Year Later*

No one was more excited to celebrate the nuptials of Carter Biggles-Vanderhousen and Georgia Brubaker than Georgia's uncle, Big Daddy Brubaker. So when his wayfaring niece finally returned from the adventure with Harlan's son, not only in love, but having seen justice served in the matter of the Klondike case, both Big Daddy and his brother, Tiny, were overjoyed.

For a full year, practically everyone in the Brubaker clan was involved with the planning and execution of the sensational ceremony. Especially Ginny and Carolina. Though their weddings had been magical in their own ways, they'd hardly been full of the fanfare that was heralding Georgia's impending marriage.

The wedding was planned to fall at the end of Big Daddy Brubaker's annual family reunion. A week of incredible festivities were planned, including a number of popular headliners from the country-western music circuit. It was wonderful, enchanting and, for Georgia, who'd been waiting a year to be married, interminable.

And so, finally, on a sultry, late-summer evening on the last Saturday of the reunion, Georgia Brubaker became Mrs. Carter Biggles-Vanderhousen. The formal ceremony—held in the conservatory—was everything Georgia had ever dreamed it would be from the time she was old enough to play wedding with her sisters and their cousins.

The reception was held immediately following, on the veranda. An orange harvest moon rose as the band played. The dance floor was filled with the couples that made up Georgia's life. From time to time she'd feel a glimmer of déjà vu, for—with the exception of the mobsters arguing at the bar—the party was eerily similar to the one where she and Carter had first danced together.

Only, this time Georgia was a married woman.

As she swayed to the music in the arms of her husband, she glanced around, tears of joy brimming in her eyes. Big Daddy and Miss Clarise danced alternately with each other and with their grandchildren, whose numbers now exceeded the passel they'd raised. Bru's oldest would be entering high school this fall, a fact that rendered the two weepy over the sonic speed with which time had passed.

Georgia's oldest sister, Ginny, danced with her husband, Colt, while one of their nieces baby-sat their three-month-old son, Austin. Her other newly married sister, Carolina, sat this dance out, as she and her husband, Hunt, were expecting their first baby anyday now.

Harlan and Daisy were cutting the rug to bits alongside Ted and Mary and the rest of the campers from the lake. Blessedly, Barb had left the music to the professionals.

It was a night for celebration. For laughter and family. A night for lovers.

"When do you think we can bust outta here?" Georgia leaned back in Carter's arms as they danced to a mellow jazz number in the middle of the dance floor. Unlike her sisters, Georgia had wanted a dream wedding, and had been willing to wait for it. However, it had been a year now, and she was itching to get started on the honeymoon.

"Well, why don't you set something on fire and we can sneak off unnoticed?"

Georgia's mischievous smile reflected her husband's. "That's not very friendly."

"That's because I'm saving my friendliness for you." Carter nuzzled her neck and murmured, "Speaking of setting something on fire…"

"Mmm. Oh, yeah…" Georgia's eyes slid closed. "In that case, I suggest that we hightail it out of here before we have to endure anoth—"

A hand at her elbow stopped her midsentence. "May we cut in?"

Battling back her impatience, Georgia looked up to find Brandon and Bunny standing beside them, smiles of congratulations lighting their expressions.

"Brandon, old boy, you are hardly my type." Carter sighed, but stopped dancing. He and Georgia exchanged beleaguered glances.

"Then, I'll settle for a dance with the bride."

"Make it quick, man. This is my wedding night." He turned to Bunny. "Dance?"

Bunny nodded. "I'd love to." Her newly found self-confidence was clearly due to Brandon's affection.

As Brandon took Georgia in his arms, she looked longingly after her groom.

"I'm going to ask her to marry me."

The sudden declaration had Georgia's head snapping around. She peered into Brandon's face. "You *are?* You are going to ask *Bunny* to *marry* you?"

"Actually, she prefers to be called Matilda now, and yes, I am."

*"When?"*

"Soon."

Georgia squealed and hugged Brandon, drawing curious looks from her guests. "Oh, Brandon, after what my sisters and I put you through last year! To know that you have found true love, well that's just wonderful. I'm so happy for you."

Her enthusiastic embrace had him grinning. "Yeah, well, I guess you Brubaker girls just weren't meant to fall for the boy next door."

"Matilda's a lucky woman."

"I'm the lucky one."

Radiating joy for each other, they reminisced for a bit and pondered the future for a while, but finally, unable to stay away from his bride another moment, Carter returned Bunny to Brandon and pulled Georgia into his arms.

"Not sorry you married me instead of Brandon?"

"Hardly."

With a steely arm at the small of her back, he drew her close for a long, heartfelt kiss. "Good."

The low strains of cool jazz filled the air, underscored by the sounds of the Moorlands' car backfiring, which echoed through the woods as the elderly couple headed for home. Seemingly in celebration of the wedding, the crickets' serenade was more full-bodied than usual, and Clarabella's cowbell jangled from where she stood at the bottom of the stairs, placidly munching on the sprawling lawn.

The old girl had become something of a pet dog, as Georgia couldn't bear the idea of parting with her, let alone eating her. And since Big Daddy could never deny the "little gals" in his family anything, he built the bag of bones a little barn behind the garage, complete with a patch of lawn and put up with her occasional curious forays into the house.

"Oh, I nearly forgot to tell you," Carter murmured, as he rained kisses along her jaw. "I have a special wedding gift that I know you'll love."

"Would you stop with the gifts? We're going to need a bigger house."

"Not that kind. Bunny just told me that she heard through the medical/dental grapevine that the DNA evidence has linked Rocky Klondike to the murder of the senator. I don't think he'll be getting out of prison anytime soon. If ever."

Relief flooded Georgia, and she gripped Carter ever closer. "Oh, that is *wonderful* news! I know you're always telling me not to worry about people like him, but I'll tell you, it's a whole lot easier when you know they're behind bars."

"True." As the song came to its conclusion, Carter's gaze was drawn by a signal from across the dance floor. He sent a thumbs-up, then grabbed his wife by the hand. "C'mon, let's get out of here. Marshall is waiting out front with a car, some costumes and supplies and a couple of new identities."

"New ID? What for?"

Carter shrugged as he hustled her through the throng. "We are going to get lost for a while."

"We are? But where?" Georgia's giggles were breathless as she hustled to keep up.

"Does it matter?"

"No." Not when she was with Carter. Nothing mattered but him.

And the way he loved her.

Hands locked, they disappeared into the shadows.

With a noisy clearing of his throat and several enthusiastic taps on the microphone for the attention of the crowd, Big Daddy stood up to toast the newlyweds.

But after a moment spent holding his champagne glass aloft and searching the crowd for the faces of newlyweds, Big Daddy had to admit—much to his consternation— that they had started the honeymoon without him.

\* \* \* \* \*

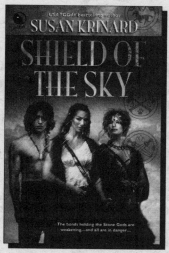

If you enjoyed what you just read,
then we've got an offer you can't resist!

# Take 2 bestselling love stories FREE!

# Plus get a FREE surprise gift!

---

**Clip this page and mail it to Silhouette Reader Service™**

**IN U.S.A.**
3010 Walden Ave.
P.O. Box 1867
Buffalo, N.Y. 14240-1867

**IN CANADA**
P.O. Box 609
Fort Erie, Ontario
L2A 5X3

**YES!** Please send me 2 free Silhouette Romance® novels and my free surprise gift. After receiving them, if I don't wish to receive anymore, I can return the shipping statement marked cancel. If I don't cancel, I will receive 4 brand-new novels every month, before they're available in stores! In the U.S.A., bill me at the bargain price of $3.57 plus 25¢ shipping and handling per book and applicable sales tax, if any*. In Canada, bill me at the bargain price of $4.05 plus 25¢ shipping and handling per book and applicable taxes**. That's the complete price and a savings of at least 10% off the cover prices—what a great deal! I understand that accepting the 2 free books and gift places me under no obligation ever to buy any books. I can always return a shipment and cancel at any time. Even if I never buy another book from Silhouette, the 2 free books and gift are mine to keep forever.

210 SDN DZ7L
310 SDN DZ7M

| Name | (PLEASE PRINT) | |
|------|----------------|---|
| Address | Apt.# | |
| City | State/Prov. | Zip/Postal Code |

*Not valid to current Silhouette Romance® subscribers.*

*Want to try two free books from another series?*
*Call 1-800-873-8635 or visit www.morefreebooks.com.*

\* Terms and prices subject to change without notice. Sales tax applicable in N.Y.
\*\* Canadian residents will be charged applicable provincial taxes and GST.
  All orders subject to approval. Offer limited to one per household.
  ® are registered trademarks owned and used by the trademark owner and or its licensee.

SROM04R                                    ©2004 Harlequin Enterprises Limited

# More Than Words

*Ordinary women...extraordinary compassion*

Harlequin celebrates the lives of women who give back to their communities. Five bestselling authors come together in MORE THAN WORDS, a collection of fictional romantic stories inspired by these dedicated women.

These entertaining stories will warm your heart and lift your spirits.

**All net proceeds from this book will be reinvested in Harlequin's charity work.**

*Available October 2004 at your local retailer.*

HARLEQUIN

*More Than Words*

**Visit www.HarlequinMoreThanWords.com**

SILHOUETTE *Romance*®

# COMING NEXT MONTH

**#1742 RICH MAN, POOR BRIDE—Linda Goodnight**
*In a Fairy Tale World...*
Ruthie Ellsworthy Fernandez is determined to steer clear of gorgeous military physician Diego Vargas and his wandering ways. Ruthie wants roots, a home and a family more than anything, and though Diego's promises are tempting, they're only temporary—aren't they?

**#1743 DADDY IN THE MAKING—Sharon De Vita**
Danger is Michael Gallagher's middle name. But when he comes to a rural Wisconsin inn to unwind and lay low, beautiful innkeeper Angela DiRosa and her adorable daughter charm their way into his life. And soon Michael is finding that risking his heart is the most dangerous adventure of all.

**#1744 THE BOWEN BRIDE—Nicole Burnham**
Can a wedding dress made from magical fabric guarantee a lasting marriage? That's what Katie Schmidt wonders about her grandmother's special thread. And when handsome single father Jared Porter walks into Katie's bridal shop, she wonders if the magic is strong enough to weave this wonderful man into her life for good.

**#1745 A WHIRLWIND...MAKEOVER—Nancy Lavo**
Maddie Sinclair is a walking disaster! But when she needs a date to her high school reunion, her friend Dan Willis uses his photographer's eye to transform her from mousy to magnificent. With her new looks, Maddie's turning heads...especially Dan's.

SRCNM1004